THE LOYAL WIFE

A gripping psychological thriller with a twist

NATALIE BARELLI

The Last Word
NSW Australia
Paperback ISBN: 978-0-6482259-3-5
eBook ISBN: 978-0-6482259-4-2

Cover design by coverquill.com

Also by Natalie Barelli

Until I Met Her *(The Emma Fern Series Book 1)*

After He Killed Me *(The Emma Fern Series Book 2)*

Missing Molly

Chapter One

I never thought I'd end up in a place like this. I never thought I'd end up in a *house* like this. I still get a little thrill when I drive up to my beautiful home, with its large front porch framed by four enormous white columns. It might not be the most expensive house around here, but it sure ain't the cheapest.

But hey, I deserve it. Mike may be the money guy, but I'm the perfect wife. Take this evening, for instance. We hosted a small dinner party that was very important to Mike, and by extension, to me.

It was a success. I may not have cooked the food myself, we have Sophia, our housekeeper/cook for that, but I do know how to plan the right menu for the right occasion, and I know how to be the perfect hostess.

We invited Rob and Bethany Wolfe into our home because they're rich, interested in Mike's work, and right now he needs campaign donors. I don't know why, exactly. I mean, we're pretty rich ourselves, I would have thought he could pay for his own campaign, but what do I know?

Mike runs his own boutique investment firm, and he's

done extremely well, and I do mean, *extremely* well. Then one day, a couple years ago, he announced that it was time he got involved in politics, and he has set his eyes on the prize: governor. I've been very encouraging, because I think it would be nice to be governor's wife. It has a certain ring to it.

He says he needs to make himself more visible. Enter Rob and Bethany Wolfe, with their deep pocket and keen interests in state affairs. That's what they call it: 'state affairs,' as if they actually mean 'affairs of the state' instead of 'you scratch my back and I'll scratch yours and we'll call it lobbying.'

Along with Rob and Bethany, we also asked the Porters —Larry and Janis—because they're also rich, and Larry told Mike that he sometimes plays golf with Rob, so what better way to break the ice but to be among friends.

By the time dessert arrived—white chocolate cheese cake with raspberry coulis—Bethany Wolfe was adamant this had been the best crab soup she'd *ever* tasted (it's the dry sherry that makes all the difference) and Rob insisted the seared duck with pickled red cabbage and truffle cream would be the death of him.

"I sure hope not," I quipped. "You haven't contributed anything yet!" He guffawed till he was red in the face. Mike beamed at me, and his handsome face and crinkled smile made me feel all warm and tingly.

"Oh by the way, Tamra," Janis Porter said as we accompanied them to the door, "I almost forgot!" She reached into her bag and pulled out a small white envelope, handed it to me.

"Of course! Larry's wedding! How lovely. You must be so proud." I knew already that Janis was bringing the invitation to their son's wedding. But what brought me a small rush of pleasure was that it was addressed to Mr. & Mrs. Mike Mitchell in elegant script.

Mrs. Mike Mitchell. That's me. Well, my name is Tamra but even after six years of marriage, I still get a thrill when people call me Mrs. Mike Mitchell. Not that it happens *that* often. Folks are pretty relaxed around here, even if we live in one of the nicest neighborhoods of Greensboro.

I'm still thinking about that as I help Sophia put things away in the kitchen. Mike has already gone upstairs to get ready for bed. He doesn't like it that I do that, but I can't help it. It's late, Sophia will want to get home, and it won't take long to tidy up if it's the two of us.

When she's finally left, I turn out all the lights and make my way up the stairs. I'm smiling to myself, knowing that I did a fine job tonight and Mike will be thrilled. We'll stay up a while, no doubt, chatting in bed, going over the evening in minute detail, then we'll turn out the light and Mr. and Mrs. Mike Mitchell will get down to an altogether different business.

And then he'll snore softly beside me, and I won't be able to sleep because fucking Madison is coming home tomorrow.

Chapter Two

Madison is home.

She parks her little Audi next to my SUV just as I open the trunk to get the groceries out. I plaster on a smile and ignore the flutter of anxiety in my stomach as I walk over and pull my stepdaughter in a hug—or try to. She's so stiff and unresponsive it's more like hugging a plank. I can feel the bones jutting out from every angle. When I release her, I keep one hand on her bony shoulder for a better look. She shrugs my hand away.

"How did the exams go?" I ask. What I *really* want to ask is, *when's the last time you ate?*

"Fine, good."

"Wow! That's great news! Hey, can you give me a hand with these bags?" I sound like I'm auditioning for the role of the super-bouncy stepmom in a super-bouncy family sitcom.

We split the load and go inside the house. Immediately, and as usual, an awkward silence befalls us. I don't know how to have a conversation with Madison. Even when she helps me put the food away, her gestures are heavy with

4

reluctance. Or maybe I'm just imagining it. Maybe it's my fault.

In my distant memory, it wasn't always like this. A few short years ago, she would let her guard down, and we would share a laugh. Now whenever that happens, she'll catch herself and sneer at me. As if the joke was on me.

She pulls out the packet of granola I picked out for her. "Why did you get this? I don't eat this, it's gross. So full of sugar."

"Well, I do," I lie.

She eyes me up and down. "Figures."

I grab it from her and slam it on the counter, and she jumps.

"Jeez, Tamra! What's up with you?"

Now I feel guilty. Already. How long did that take? Ten minutes? "Forget it." I reach a hand out to her and pat her on the shoulder before she shrugs off my touch.

"Sorry, Madison. I have a lot on my mind. Tell me about college."

She continues to put the rest of the groceries away, as if I hadn't spoken. I sigh.

Madison is in her second year of a business management degree at Columbia. She's actually really bright—smarter than either of her brothers. She's also fiercely independent, which I'm secretly quite impressed by. She shares a small apartment in Midtown with one of her girlfriends, and Mike contributes a little money toward her expenses, but less and less each month because she has a part-time job. She is gradually shouldering more of the rent and told him that next semester she won't need his help anymore, although she did let him buy her that little Audi. Her mother lives in Connecticut now, and no doubt she pitches in, too.

"You've lost a bit of weight," I tell her, and confirm right there what a moron I am. She's disturbingly thin. Saying she's lost a bit of weight isn't just pointing out the bleeding obvious; I sound like I'm making fun of her.

"Whatever. I'm going to take my stuff to my room, okay?"

"Of course."

And she's gone.

We don't have children together, Mike and I. He has three fully grown ones from his previous marriage, and he didn't want to go through all that again. What he *actually* said, when I brought up the possibility of having kids early on in our marriage, was that he didn't want to share me with anyone.

I knew what he meant, but still—I thought it was a really sweet way of putting it.

Madison is his youngest. She has two older brothers, Jack and Zach. We don't see them much but that's only because they have their own lives, far away from here.

Madison was fourteen when Mike and I became engaged. I used to fantasize about the kind of relationship she and I would have. I was going to be like a wise older sister to her. I could advise her about all sorts of stuff, like fashion: can you get away with Tartan? Probably not. Boyfriends: should you have sex on the first date? Hell, yeah. I couldn't wait.

Even before I met her, Mike would tell me wonderful things about her. "Maddie has a real big heart, she's a real sweet girl. You'll see."

I imagined her growing up as a young woman under my watchful eye (even though she only lived with us some weekends and half the summer). I'd help her with her homework, make sure she got good grades. I could picture myself beating pancake mix on a Sunday morning, the large white bowl tucked securely under my arm while I whisked and talked at the same time, a pretty apron fitted around my waist.

"How's school going, Maddie? Do you need help with your homework?" I'd ask, and she'd be sitting at the kitchen table biting the end of her pencil, struggling with her English essay. And because she was so kind, she'd take a year off before starting medical school to travel to third-world countries as part of a volunteer program. I imagined her receiving some incredibly important international award for her good works, Mike and I in the audience looking on, proud as Punch. In her acceptance speech, she would thank me, from the bottom of her heart, for inspiring her, and then we would go on *Oprah* together.

I'm such a loser.

She's a young woman now, and she hates me. She thinks it's my fault her parents split up, no matter how many times I've told her that they were going through a separation when I met her father. "Yeah, right," she'd snort.

But now, she's in college studying for an MBA, "just like Daddy." Once, I told her that I, too, have an MBA. And that mine has *with honors* attached to it. I didn't mean to lie, it just came out, because in that moment I was sick of feeling excluded by the two of them, but it didn't matter, anyway. She merely shrugged. "Whatever," she replied, reminding me that I don't count.

I hear the front door close, and I'm relieved that Mike is home. Madison runs down the stairs, and I push myself away from the kitchen counter and walk out into the entryway just as she throws her arms around his neck, like a little girl again.

"Daddy!" she squeals in a voice too high-pitched for her age.

His face lights up at the sight of her. Funnily enough, I've never been jealous of their relationship. Good luck to her. She's lucky to be loved like that—by both her parents, I might add. Someone wise once said you can always pick the people who were loved as children. I used to think it was because they'd be confident and really well adjusted. Now I know it's because they're so fucking spoiled.

Mike throws his jacket on the back of a chair and in moments, they've settled themselves in the living room. He, getting comfortable and rolling up his shirt sleeves, she with her legs curled up under her. He calls her princess and asks about her studies. She tells him she's enrolled in a new area of focus called *Decisions and Risks Analysis,* and that's what she wants to specialize in. It's been a hard decision because she just *loves* everything in the curriculum. He nods sagely and tells her it's a good choice. He says he'll have a place for her when she gets home next year, not in his office because that would be nepotism, but a good place in a good firm. She knows it already. He's told her fifty-thousand times, she says, laughing.

Why can't she talk to me like that? I asked the same questions in the kitchen this afternoon, but all I got was an impatient shrug.

Upstairs in our bedroom, I tell myself to let it go. It's only because she's just arrived that her attitude gets to me. I'll get used to it in a day or two. I always do. Sort of.

"Hey."

Mike sneaks up to me from behind and wraps his arms around my waist. I lean my head back against his shoulder and let my body sink into him.

"Hey yourself," I whisper, closing my eyes. He kisses the side of my neck. I take in the scent of him and smile. He smells terrible, and that's all my fault.

It was our third date, and I was already obsessed with him. I thought of nothing and no-one else. I'd stopped at Crabtree Valley Mall to pick up some of my favorite perfume, and on impulse I bought him a bottle of after-shave because I liked the ad. I liked it because the guy jumping from plane to sports car to dinner date reminded of Mike. I was flushed with too much wine and coyness when I gave it to him over dinner. He smiled, that gorgeous, sexy, knock my knees together crooked smile, and he kissed me.

I have since become aware that back then I had no taste, and that cheap bottle of aftershave was the last thing he would have wanted. Lord knows I've since splurged on the most expensive kind imaginable, but every now and then I'll find he's bought himself that one again, just to wear occasionally, privately almost, because it reminds him of me, he says.

"What, cheap?" I'd joked when he told me.

"That the girl I married thinks I can jump from plane to sports car to dinner table," he'd replied.

So, I let him wear it. Very occasionally. Privately.

"You're excited about tonight?" he asks now.

"Of course not. Why the heck should I be?" I reply. He laughs softly into my hair.

"I'm going to have a shower," he says, releasing me, and I smile, pretend to rearrange things on the top of the dresser while in the mirror I watch my husband undress.

Chapter Three

It's funny, the details that pop into your mind at the precise moment your life changes, isn't it?

When I picked up Mike's trousers from the bed just now, and I felt something in his pocket, I didn't think anything of it. I thought it was a Kleenex. Then I pulled out the lace panties, and I held them up, staring at them dangling from my index finger, and for some completely unknown reason, I thought to myself, *that blue would look lovely for the drapes in the living room.* Then I clenched my teeth, scrunched them up, and curled my fingers into a fist until it hurt.

To be fair, it's a very nice blue. Soft and powdery, more sky than lavender. I turn my gaze toward the door of the master bathroom. I can hear the shower running, and I imagine Mike—his eyes closed, oblivious to the wave of fury welling up in the next room.

Really?

I relax my fist and let them unfurl in my palm. I hold the thong between two fingers. Nothing to it, really. It's so light and delicate, silk probably, and so small it's hard to imagine what purpose it serves, other than to titillate. I should be wearing something like that. Did he buy it for her? Whoever she may be? Did he order it online from Victoria's Secret or some such place? Did she unwrap it from its soft paper, smile, and disappear for a little while, only to come back moments later wearing nothing but... this?

It should have been me he bought this for.

I clench my jaw so hard my teeth hurt. Then I take hold of the panties in both hands and pull hard at the fabric. I let out a grunt as I yank at both ends with all my strength, but they're made of sturdier stuff and all I have to show for my efforts is a red welt on my knuckle, where the delicately sewn, silky edge, cut into my skin. I even try to tear them up with my teeth until it dawns on me she would have worn them before he stuffed them in his pocket. I spit them out, quickly wipe my tongue with the back of my hand.

I sit on the bed, defeated, still clutching the panties, and bring my knuckle to my lips to soothe the pain. Then I catch sight of myself in the mirror above the vanity. The corners of my mouth are pulling downward. I look old and mean. I lift a hand against my cheek; my skin feels dry. I turn my face this way and that. Actually, I don't look that bad. I like the way I've done my hair, in a loose chignon with strands framing my face. Mike likes my hair that way too. I look okay, not amazing, more getting-older-trophy-wife than catwalk model material, but some men like that. Men like Mike. God. Who am I kidding? I've let myself go, that's the problem. Is it time to get work done? Damn right, it is.

I wonder what *she* looks like. Not thirty-three years old, I'll bet. The last *indiscretion* had been, what? Twenty? Only two years older than Madison. That's pretty fucked up when you think about it.

Which I do. Often.

The bathroom door opens, and I immediately drop the panties to the floor, shoving them under the bed with the heel of my foot while rearranging my face into a benign expression.

"Hey, baby doll, you're ready?" he says, throwing that crooked smile at me. I don't answer. I pretend to be fussing with the buttons on my cream satin shirt.

Mike pulls the belt of his bathrobe tighter and picks up his phone from the top of the dresser. "Rob called, I forgot to tell you." His thumb quickly flicks over the screen.

Is it her? Has she texted him?

"He asked me to thank you for an excellent dinner last night," he says.

A terrible thought occurs to me. Could the panties belong to Bethany? Or Janis? *Oh, shut up, Tamra. Now you've really lost it.* Bethany Wolfe is sixty years old. Heck, some people can wear that age, but Bethany sure ain't one of them. She's had so much *work* done that you literally can no longer tell if she's smiling or crying, happy or sad. It's all one death-mask to her.

Janis, on the other hand, is nothing like that. I like Janis. She has a big laugh, big hair, and a big heart. But she's also at least twenty years too old and as many pounds too heavy for that little blue number.

No. The owner of that skimpy bit of frill is no more than, oh, twenty-two, maybe, very thin, lithe and ... *oh, shut up, Tamra.*

"You're all right?" Mike asks behind me.

"What? Oh fine, just thinking about last night."

"I'm going to get dressed." He puts his phone down

12

and disappears inside the walk-in closet. I sprint over to the dresser to try and catch it before the lock screen comes on. Too late.

I should have been screaming at him. I should have slapped his face by now. I should have—what?

I have no family nearby, my friends are just as much his friends, and he's a lot more influential than I am. I could storm off and go to stay with Dwayne and Lauren. I know she'll help me, but she's only around the corner. That would be silly. What's left? Hotels? Then what?

Maybe I should go back to work. Except I have no skills. When I met him, I worked for an accounting firm. Behind the reception desk.

We met in the elevator. He was carrying a small square case, like a miniature suitcase, on wheels. It made me laugh, a tall strong man like him, pulling this ridiculously small bag.

"What the heck have you got in there? Gold bullions?"

I liked that word, bullion. I only just learnt it the day before and I was pleased to have placed it so quickly.

He looked down at his case and then at me, and gave me that crooked smile of his, his lips curled up on one side. I fell in love, right there and then.

I was on my way to grab a take-out coffee for my boss, and he came with me. Just like that. Without even asking, or being asked.

"Where do you work?" he said.

"Carrington & Denton. Accountants. You know them?"

"Nope, but I wish I did. You're the most beautiful accountant I ever met."

I didn't correct him. I liked that he'd assumed I was that smart. On the way back, I went to the parking lot with him, and we had sex in the front seat of his BMW. Then I retrieved the Styrofoam cup of lukewarm coffee from the roof of his car, waved my fingers, and went back to work, thinking I'd never see him again, but it was nice, anyway.

I rub my fingers on my temples, trying to stop the looming headache in its tracks. I need to think this through. Who the heck is she, anyway? I'm dying here. It's not just that we have been here before, Mike and I, but that it was never *ever* supposed to happen again. That's what he said, when he cried and begged and promised. Especially after everything we went through back then. We did things that I don't even want to think about to get him out of a shockingly bad situation, all because Mike Mitchell decided to follow his penis instead of his brain. In fact, I've tried so hard not to think about it anymore that it had just started to feel like it never happened.

Except now we're here again. Really?

Mike emerges, looking handsome in his chinos and linen-blend polo, his dark hair still damp. He snaps his Movado watch on and looks at me.

"Are you ready?"

"Almost. Give me a minute." I stand up and brush down my skirt—for something to do—and I go to the bathroom to cry.

Chapter Four

We're off to church this evening, the three of us. I'm about to get in the car, one hand on top of the passenger door, when I hear Madison behind me.

"Can I sit in the front?"

"Sit in the back, Maddie," Mike says.

"But I'm not feeling well!" she whines.

I glance at Mike above the car. An apologetic smile is already reaching his eyes. "Do you mind?"

Damn right, I mind. "We're not going far, she'll be fine," I say.

"Dad?"

"You know she gets carsick, Tamra."

I won't win this battle. Not the second day of Madison's vacation. "Fine, whatever."

Madison hasn't been carsick since she was a kid. But these are the little things she does to make me feel excluded. The third wheel. As usual, Mike is oblivious. Or at least I think he is.

We've settled in and are ready to go when he mumbles something about forgetting something. I wonder if it's the blue panties. I look up at the window of our bedroom on the first floor, imagining him reaching for the trousers folded neatly on the back of the chair, and going quickly through the pockets, only to realize they're not there. They're gone. The evidence of his crimes has disappeared. No, not really, it's just that he doesn't know where it is, anymore.

He comes out again, doing a quick jog down the porch steps.

"Did you find it?" I ask, sweetly.

He pats the pocket of his blazer as he settles back into the driver seat.

"Yep, I wanted to show Pastor Frank the letter from the Chronicle. I'm glad I remembered."

I have no idea what letter he's talking about, but as the rain begins to fall on the windshield, I wonder if he's forgotten already about the panties in his pocket.

"How was work today?" I ask.

"Fine, good. Busy."

I bet.

"You look nice," he says to Madison. No, she doesn't. She looks tired, thin. "Yeah, you do," I concur, from my third-wheel position in the backseat.

"Thanks Dad," she says. "I'm excited about tonight. I'm so pleased I could be here for it."

"Me too, princess."

Pastor Frank has asked Mike to speak tonight, because Mike and I are making a significant donation to the church, but really, we're launching his campaign. Until an hour ago, I, too, was excited about tonight, even though I wasn't crazy about the fact Madison would be here, too. Now my nails are digging in the soft flesh of my palms.

I catch Mike looking at me in the rearview mirror.

"You're okay?" he asks.

"Yes, why?"

"No reason."

Madison chats away, the rain stops as quickly as it came, and five minutes later, we pull into the parking lot.

"Great, Rob Wolfe is here," Mike says.

Fuck Rob Wolfe, I think.

"Hello, Tamra, how lovely to see you again so soon!" Bethany purrs.

I kiss her cold cheek. "Hello, Bethany. It's good of you to come!"

"Well, we didn't want to miss it!" Bethany says. "Hello, Madison. You look nice! Are you looking forward to tonight?"

"Oh yes, we are," she replies, looking at her father. "Dad loves the opportunity to introduce himself to the people of our fine state. He says it's going to be the best part of the campaign."

Cue vomit.

"We'll see you in there," Mike tells them as he takes my hand on one side, and Madison's hand in the other, and leads us inside.

I like going to this church. When I was a kid, before my mom left us, we used to go to a church not unlike this one, except smaller. There was always a band performing live on stage, and we'd stand and sing and receive God, and it made us happy. Happy Clappers, they called us.

"A gift from our Lord!" Pastor Frank thunders from the stage, holding up the oversized novelty check for twenty-thousand dollars signed by Mike and me. Everyone laughs, because we all know God doesn't carry a check book.

Pastor Frank walks up and down the stage still holding up his check. It makes him look like a game show host. He asks the congregation if we know how lucky we are to have in our midst such a good Christian? Such an upstanding family man who is proud of his old-fashioned values? But then Pastor Frank explains that it's not about the money, it's the miracle of community and love for one another that we are celebrating here, today.

"Mike Mitchell told me, more than once, that the most important things in life are God, family, and community. These might seem like old-fashioned values to some, although not to anyone in this room." Cue more laughter as Pastor Frank makes an expansive gesture toward the audience. Then, more soberly, he adds, "But make no mistakes. These values are what this very church is built upon, and they are what makes our country great. And now, thanks to the generous support of Mike and Tamra Mitchell, we can continue the important work we do here! Thank you, Sir! You're a good man!" He shouts the last part, and the sound distorts and bounces around the walls.

The applause is genuine and generous. These people are kind and gracious, smiling and nodding in our direction and I think to myself, *how can he sit here and not blush with shame?*

"Come on up, Mike!" Pastor Frank bellows into the microphone. Mike beams at me, then at Madison. He gets up and plants a kiss on her cheek, then mine. I resist the urge to rub the kiss off and move my legs sideways to let him pass.

For the next fifteen minutes, I sit here and listen to him pontificate about all the great things he wants to do for our great community. He goes on and on about family, loyalty, promises, and faith. I want to stand up and pull the panties from my back pocket in a grand gesture and shout, "Oh, really? What's this then?"

They're not in my back pocket, obviously. They're under the bed. I shut my eyes tightly to stop myself from crying. It's people like Mike who give religion a bad name. I don't care what he says, or how often he prays, he's just *using* God to get where he wants. But what slices at my heart isn't just his infidelity, it's that I protected him, that I heard his promises and I thought they were real. I can't believe I've been so stupid. Maybe he truly is evil, and I'm the only one who knows it.

Outside now, we chat with everyone, shake hands, receive and give good words, words of God, words of wisdom, words of neighborly love. Normally, this would be my time to catch up with neighbors. We'd be discussing the next block party, or whose turn it is to host the next book club meeting. I'd be asking Marylin about her daughter Isabelle who has been causing her such trouble lately. *Teenagers! Who'd have them!* And I'd chat with Mel and Graham, ask to hold little Benjamin, because I always do. *Just look at this little face*, I would coo, while he gripped my finger into his tiny little hand. Then I'd ask Mel if he was feeding better now, because I know how stressful it's been for her. Jeanie would want to know if I'm going to tennis with the others on Thursday, and normally I'd tell her yes, of course, like I always do. Then we'd laugh.

But not tonight. Tonight, I am too embarrassed to speak with anyone, in case they can see it my face.

Oh, he's been playing around, has he? We always knew it would never last. It's not like you're one of us, really, is it?

"Hey, you," says a voice behind me. I turn and smile at Lauren and give her a warm hug.

"This is nice," I say. She's wearing a charming green

silk suit: a pencil skirt and cute little jacket with an emerald necklace. "Is it new?"

"No, but I'm taking it out for air."

"It suits you."

"Thanks, girlfriend! So, that was nice, about Mike, what the pastor said."

I look away, involuntarily rolling my eyes. She takes a step back and cocks her head. "Everything okay?"

"Sure, why?"

She waves her hand in front of her face as if flapping my lies away. "What's going on?"

I shake my head. "Nothing. I'm in a funny mood. You're right, it was great."

But Lauren won't let go. She's that kind of person, and now I wish I hadn't made a face. She moves closer and narrows her eyes a little. "Tell me."

"There's nothing, I swear."

"Cross your heart?"

I smile. "I'll tell you another day. Is Dwayne here?"

"He was, but he had to leave. Can I get a lift back with you?"

"Sure." *You can sit in the back with me.* "Where did he go?"

This time it's her turn to roll her eyes. "He's going away on business tonight. Honestly, sometimes I suspect Dwayne has another family somewhere he's not telling me about. He's away from home so much, I'm worried I'll forget what he looks like."

I laugh. "You always exaggerate."

She's about to say something else but stops herself and smiles at someone behind me.

"Good evening, Tamra."

I turn and smile at Pastor Frank.

"I'm returning your husband." He clasps Mike's shoulder, then takes my hand in both of his. "Very nice to see you."

"Thank you, Pastor."

"Did you enjoy the sermon?"

"I did."

"Good. You're welcome," he says, still smiling with teeth whiter than snow, and the fact that he's not thanking *me* does not go unnoticed.

"I hope our gift will make a difference to the people who need it most, Pastor Frank." I hook my arm into Mike's as I say this, looking like an angel.

"It most certainly will." He closes his eyes for a few seconds, like some kind of benevolent guru lost in prayer, I don't know. Pastor Frank gives me the creeps. When he opens his eyes again, he smiles at Lauren who has been standing there like an asparagus.

"Hello, Lauren," Mike says. He only says it because Pastor Frank is here.

She lifts an eyebrow and extends her hand. "Well, hello to you too, Mike, congratulations, lovely speech."

"Thank you," he mumbles, barely audible.

"And hello again, you," Lauren hugs Madison warmly.

I look from one to the other. "Again?"

"Maddie came by yesterday, to say hi," she says.

"Really? When?" I can't help it. Madison *adores* Lauren, which is really weird. After all, her dad isn't a fan, and Lauren is *my* friend. Sometimes, I suspect that it's a ploy to outdo me, some weird shit like, *she may be your friend, but she likes me best. What does that say about you?* And yet, I try so much harder than Lauren does. Whenever I bring it up, she says I'm over-thinking it. That I'm being too sensitive.

"On the way, I dropped in on Lauren before I got home," Madison replies in a bored tone.

"Good! That's nice." I say, not meaning it. I turn to Mike. "By the way, we're giving Lauren a lift home."

"Of course." He even manages to smile at her.

Mike doesn't like Lauren, and sometimes I wonder if it's only because Lauren doesn't fawn all over him like most women, and also because she's not particularly useful to him. I prefer not to have them together in the same room if I can help it, because Mike will be rude somehow, and I'll get embarrassed. But Lauren either doesn't notice or doesn't care.

Pastor Frank brings the photographer over. "It's for the newsletter," he says. Mike, Madison, and I pose obligingly, then it's Mike and Pastor Frank's turn, and finally the four of us, with Pastor Frank holding the oversized novelty check.

"What's he doing here?" Mike whispers to Pastor Frank. We all follow Mike's gaze and our eyes land on Brad King, talking to the Wolfes, no less.

"Don't worry about him," Pastor Frank says with a shake of the head.

"He's announced his candidacy, did you know?"

"I heard. Trust me, Mike, you've got nothing to worry about."

So Brad King is running against Mike for governor. It's news to me. I can see why Mike's annoyed about that. Brad King is a big businessman in the area, and he employs an awful lot of people. Plus, he has a lot of charisma, which doesn't hurt, but then again so does Mike. In spades. Still, I can't help but feel a little cheered up at his discomfort. Then there's the incumbent. I mean, North Carolina already has a governor, and he's doing just fine. It occurs to me that Mike is actually a long way from office.

"He's got a nerve. This isn't even his church," Mike mutters, still staring.

Pastor Frank pats him on the back. "Don't worry about it."

But I watch Mike struggling to hold back his anger, and it's not easy. His career is the most important thing in his life, of course. All that crap about family values and community is bullshit, and if I didn't know that before, I do now. They're just lines he tosses out to help him get where he wants. The most important things to Mike are not *God, family, and community*, they're *Mike, Money, and Power*.

Chapter Five

Patti looks up at me through her ugly, thin-rimmed glasses. She's such a strange woman, she makes my skin crawl. She always sits up really straight, like she's the quintessential, well-behaved secretary. Like she takes *pride* in being Mike Mitchell's personal assistant, when everyone knows that just means she picks up his laundry and books restaurants for his lunches. I've never had concerns about her because, frankly, she's not his type. I can't see that she's anyone's type, in fact, but she must be because she's married—to a guy equally as weird, I might add—as I found out at the last Christmas party.

She always wears some super-modest outfit, and today, true to form, she's got on a buttoned-up pale-yellow shirt with a round, decorative collar and a pair of corduroy pants. It could be an uber-cool street fashion outfit on someone else—maybe, at a stretch—but on her it just looks like she's going for some kind of *demure* look and ends up looking just weird. I honestly cannot picture her wearing that blue piece of nothing, nor would I want to.

"Hello, Tamra. Were we expecting you?"

We.

Patti has worked for Mike for three years, and she is quite the lioness protecting her cubs when it comes to access. Sometimes that's annoying. Some days if I call to check his schedule, she'll pause for a moment, as if pondering whether it's appropriate to tell me. Or maybe I'm just imagining it.

"Hi, Patti. No, don't get up, please. How are you?"

She sits back down slowly. "Very well, Tamra. But Mike isn't here."

"Oh, right. What a shame. I wanted to surprise him, take him out to lunch."

She raises an eyebrow—understandably, since I've never done that before.

"You should have called, made an appointment." Then I guess she remembers who I am because she flashes a toothy smile.

"Yeah, I know. It's just that sometimes it's a good idea to be impulsive, you know, keep the romance alive, don't you think?" I wink at her, which makes her blush. I look around the office, trying to spot the owner of a size-small blue thong, but no one stands out. They're mostly guys who work here.

"When will he be back?"

She glances at her computer screen. "Not before three, at the earliest."

I wonder if he's with *her*. I lean forward, trying to catch a glimpse of the schedule. She quickly swivels the monitor away, just an inch, before adding, "Strategic meeting, over at headquarters."

I nod.

"Was there anything in particular?"

"Not really, no." I perch on a corner of her desk. She

widens her eyes and quickly moves things around the desk to make room for me. Or to protect her stuff from me, I can't tell.

"Tell me, Patti, anyone new in the gang? Anyone joined up the cause lately? As an intern, perhaps?" I take another look around, craning my neck a little to see above the computer screens dotted about the place.

"Hum, no, I don't— except for—"

Aha. I knew it.

"—Johnathan in the mailroom, why? Has Mike said anything? Because I —"

"No," I sigh. "Mike hasn't said anything. I was just wondering."

"Are you all right, Tamra? You seem a bit jumpy."

I play with the paperclips in the small bowl on her desk, then I lean forward and blurt out, in a low voice, "Do you know if Mike is fucking anyone behind my back?"

She recoils with a gasp. "Tamra!" She has her hand on her chest, like I've given her a heart attack. Suddenly, she annoys the crap out of me even more than usual, with her sanctimonious attitude and her crush on my husband. I've always known she was in love with him. She pretends it's from some kind of motherly instinct, which frankly, I find more than a little creepy. I bet she goes home at night, and, well— enough said.

I shake my head. "Sorry, Patti, I shouldn't have said that."

"Well, I…"

"I mean, I already know he's fucking someone behind my back. What I meant was, do you know who it is?"

I forgot to lower my voice, and eyes are popping above computers everywhere, eyes that only moments ago were looking down at their work, oblivious to my existence. Now, they're all trained on me.

"I think you should go, Tamra," she says sternly, averting her eyes.

"Oh wait, it's not you, Patti, is it?"

She was going to call security. To have me removed. Me. I'm his wife. His legally, lawfully, miserably wedded wife, and she wanted security to escort me. I spared her the trouble and left.

Now I sit in the car and cry, with my face in my hands. I let out great big sobs of grief because I'm frightened. I don't want my marriage to be over, but I think maybe it is.

My cell rings in my bag. I dry my cheeks with the back of my hand, drawing in puffs of air, and fish around until I find it. I answer it without looking.

"Hello?"

"Hey, girlfriend, what's happening?"

I chuckle, wiping the rest of my tears. "Hi, Lauren."

A couple of seconds pass before she says, "What's wrong?"

"Nothing, I'm fine," I wail.

"You're sounding anything but fine, Tamra. What's happened?"

"Nothing, really. I'm fine." This time I'm more in control of my voice.

"Are you sure?"

"Yes. Really, stop fussing."

She sighs. "If you say so. No, scratch that. I don't believe you, but suit yourself. Do you want to know why I called you?"

"Because you love me and you miss me?" I sniffle, wishing it was Mike on the other end.

"There's that, but I'm doing a special showing today. Come with me. I could use the help. Tell me what I should be showing off to people."

"Me? Don't be ridiculous! How would I know? You're the real estate expert."

"But you're great at everything, and especially with homey things."

Homey things. Thanks, Lauren.

"It'll be fun," she insists. "It's an amazing house."

"I don't know. I'm kinda busy today."

"I need you, Tamra!"

I sigh. "Oh, why not?"

"That's my girl."

She's not lying. The house is amazing. It's a classic colonial house—not unlike ours, in fact—but this is much, much larger. The facade is rendered so instead of the usual brick-work, it's a lovely pale gray.

"Wow. How much do they want for it?"

"One point five."

We walk up the porch, and I lay a hand on the banister, turn around, and take in the view. "Really?"

"Why, you're interested?"

I sigh. "Not right now, no."

We go through the house together, admiring the tall windows, rounded at the top, and the enormous fireplaces. It's so quiet here, even quieter than where we live.

"I'm thinking of leaving Mike," I say, apropos of nothing. I'm not looking at her. I'm studying the marble countertop.

She snorts, then laughs, then she takes in my face and she stops abruptly.

"Did I just hear you correctly?"

I look at her, and my bottom lip quivers.

"Oh, Tamra." She draws me into a tight hug, and I rest my forehead on her shoulder.

"What happened?"

I pull away. "Sorry. I shouldn't have done that now. You're working."

"Don't be silly. No one's coming for another fifteen minutes, at least. Come and cry on my shoulder. I'm glad you told me. I knew something was up. What happened?"

"Mike is having an affair."

Her hand flies to her mouth. "Are you serious? Who?"

"I don't know who." I tell her what I found, and her mouth tightens with anger.

"What a lowlife." She's so mad, I almost recoil at the force of her words. "You must come and stay with me. We'll go back to your house after this and pack your things."

I shake my head. "I can't just walk out."

"Sure, you can."

"I need to make plans."

She's about to argue, but I raise a hand, palm out. "Let me go through it my way, okay?"

She nods. "Sorry." She leans back against the counter top. "You know I'm here for you."

"I know."

"Did you tell him? That you were leaving? What did he say? Did he beg? Did he cry? Did he get on his knees and swear he would never do something like that again? You didn't believe him, I hope."

"I haven't told him anything yet. I only just found out."

"I see. When are you going to?"

I say nothing for a moment. "I wanted to wait until I had spoken to a lawyer." Then I tell her about the visit to his office and the argument with Patti. She puts her hand on her mouth, the way she does, to stifle the laughter.

"It's not funny, Lauren."

"I'm sorry, you're right." She squeezes my arm.

I sigh. "So I guess I have to tell him, because one way or another, he knows that I know."

"Hey, that's a good thing! No point in pussy-footing around. You gotta rip that Band-Aid off and get it over and done with, girlfriend."

"It's just that—"

The doorbell rings, and we both jump. She shoves a pile of brochures at me.

"Here. If anyone asks, hand them one of these and take their details down on this form."

"What? No way, I'm going home."

"No, you're not. You're helping me, remember?"

So I stay and take potential buyers through the house, and it's more fun than I imagined. It's kind of like playing house, literally. In my head I pretend it's mine. In what feels like no time at all, the viewing is over, and I help Lauren lock up.

"You should get your real estate license."

I scoff. "You must be kidding!"

"Why not? It's not that hard. I could help you, then when you pass your exam, you can come and work with me!" She beams.

I laugh. "No. I don't think so. Anyway, Mike wouldn't like it. He doesn't want me to work." Then, a short pause before I catch myself. "Oh, my God, I can't believe I just said that."

"It's none of Mike's business anymore, remember that."

"I know."

More than once, Lauren has asked me why I don't get myself a job. Don't I get bored all day alone in that great big house? Having peddled the lie—without meaning to—that I was an accountant before I met Mike, it's hard to explain why I'd get a job, say, waitressing. I couldn't exactly say it was the only skill I had, other than answering phones. So I just got into the habit of saying, *Oh, no, Mike doesn't want me to work*, because that's something people understand.

"You won't need the money, of course," she says, "because you're going to take him to the cleaners. You won't have to work a minute in your life. But it would be good for you, and I bet you'd be good at it."

We're at her car now, and I help get the brochures into the trunk. I wish I hadn't said anything.

"I wonder how Maddie will take it," she muses.

I wish she wouldn't call her 'Maddie'. I find it annoyingly intimate. Only Mike is allowed to call her Maddie, or at least that's what she says to me.

"I'm sure she'll be delighted," I mumble.

She punches me lightly on the shoulder. "Cut it out."

"You're right. Hey, have you noticed how thin she is?"

"Not particularly."

"She's bony. I don't think she eats much."

"You know what girls are like at that age. Don't you remember?"

"Not like this."

She shrugs, then brings me into her warm hug. "Let me know what I can do to help, okay? It's you I'm worried about."

31

Chapter Six

When Mike and I were dating, on a whim, I told him that in my spare time I volunteered at a charity that helped homeless women. "I just think that I'm in a privileged position, and I like to give something back. I think there should be more of that, don't you?"

He took my hand in his and kissed it softly, brushing his lips on the tips of my fingers. "You're the most remarkable woman I've ever met," he said, his eyes swimming. "I think that I'm in love with you."

So I rushed out the next day and called all the charities in the area that worked with homeless women until I found one that could use my unskilled—but unpaid—time. And a really funny thing happened: I love it. I'm actually really good at it, too. I never stopped doing it after that. Right now, I volunteer at the Catherine Duval Center for Women. It's an outreach program and I help with the paperwork, I make calls to find available beds in shelters, I help prepare food that we provide for free, and sometimes it's just a matter of being a shoulder to cry on.

A few months ago, Joan came in. She was in her fifties,

wearing what had once been an expensive coat but was now frayed at the cuffs and stained at the hem.

Her story shocked me. She had been married for thirty-odd years and had two adult children. She had never held a job, concentrating instead on being a house-wife and mother. Her husband was a lawyer, and one day he came home to tell her he was leaving. He had been having an affair with his twenty-something-year-old secretary for a few months, and they were moving in together.

Joan blamed the shock and the ensuing depression for the lack of interest she took in her own affairs. Hubby moved out and left her alone in the house—the children having long left the coop—until one day, she received an eviction notice because the house was up for sale. Joan had assumed that she would keep the house; instead, she was given seven days to ship out. Then it turned out that her name was not listed on the deed to the home. It had never been, because hubby bought it in his name, and his name only.

I was incredulous. "Didn't you ask about that? At the time?"

"I thought I was on it. I was signing whatever papers he put in front of me. I never asked because I just assumed he knew best."

To add insult to injury, over those last few months before he moved out, hubby rearranged his affairs so that on paper, he looked broke. So the house was sold from under Joan's feet, and she received not one cent from it, due to some creative accounting on the part of hubby.

"Didn't you have your own bank account?"

"What would I do with it? I didn't earn any money. We had a joint account, and not long after he moved out, my credit cards stopped working, and my access to the account had been canceled."

I couldn't fathom how one person could do that to another.

"I gave him and our children my entire adult life," she said, echoing my thoughts. I patted her knee, I hugged her, I provided Kleenex, but deep down I thought, *how could you have been so stupid?*

She wanted to know if there was any form of assistance she might be entitled to. Just to help her out, while she got herself together. "But not welfare! I wouldn't stoop this low!"

"It's not stooping," I told her. "It's a safety net. It's the mark of a good society: helping those who find themselves in a bad situation because bad things happened." Her clothes, her smell even, said everything about how she shouldn't turn her nose up at any kind of help. I gave her all the relevant information, then I put her in touch with a good lawyer.

"But I can't afford a lawyer!" she shrieked.

"You can afford this one, I promise. Call him."

Having a husband in high places has its privileges. The lawyer in question, Mario, was—and still is—somewhere between a friend and an acquaintance, and his wife and I do Pilates together. He agreed to look after Joan, pro bono. I should call Mario, find out what happened.

Now, I can't help but wonder if that's going to be me, in that tattered old chair, drying my tears on the sleeve of a scruffy coat. Because the truth is, I have no idea what our financial situation is, and where I fit in. I don't have my own money. Just the money he transfers every month into my bank account. A kind of generous allowance.

I should never have gone to his office this morning. It

was a mistake. I hadn't meant to let the cat out of the bag, so to speak, I just wanted to check out the staff. See if there might be a bright new young thing, giving me the evil eye. Now I'm puzzled why I haven't heard from Mike as I check my phone, again. He must have heard by now, about my little disturbance. I'm dreading that conversation.

I never thought we would split up. When Mike asked me to marry him, it wasn't with one knee on the ground; it was over a green salad at lunch, his eyes searching my face for reassurance, as if this moment was anything other than the happiest one of my life.

"Did you bring me a ring?" I asked, cocking my head, trying to look like it was all a joke, because otherwise I'd have burst into tears.

He grabbed the can of Diet Coke sitting on the table and pulled the ring off. "I'll get a better one, I swear, as soon as we leave here, today, now, if you promise to spend the rest of your life with me."

I still have that Coke tab ring, in a box, wrapped in soft tissue.

But all that to say, that I can't remember for the life of me where I put my copy of the prenup, although I think I remember what was in it: he keeps everything, and I can keep what I brought in. That amounts to fake diamond earrings and a whole lot of knockoff fashion. Maybe there was a clause? Some kind of consolation prize for the injured party? Isn't that how it works? It should be, if it isn't. There *should* be a clause that says that if he leaves me, I get a lot more than a Coke tab ring.

I'm going through all the shoe boxes and hat boxes that have piled up in my walk-in closet, but I can't find it. I have a little desk downstairs, a small antique thing with bowed legs and inlaid rosewood that Mike bought me for my birthday one year. He was so excited about it.

"I have a surprise," he'd said, turning me around and putting his hands over my eyes. He motioned me into the living room, and with a loud *Ta-da!,* he opened his arms wide. I took one look at it and thought, *what the heck am I supposed to do with that?* But I jumped up and down and threw my arms around his neck.

"You like it? It's Edwardian, you know."

"Is it? Wow. I hope it wasn't expensive!"

He did that little sideways flick of the head and smiled, his lips curling inward, a small but clearly self-satisfied smile. "That doesn't matter, baby doll, you know that."

It does! I want to know! What would I get for it on eBay? If it came to that?

"So now you have your own work area, somewhere to…" And I waited, face upturned, to find out what exactly was coming after that ellipsis, "…write letters, that sort of thing."

I snorted with laughter when he said that.

Now I'm staring at it, with all its cute little drawers pulled out, but the prenup isn't there. I just can't find it, and I have to know.

Inside the offices of Moller & Helms, I tell the receptionist that I want to talk to John Moller. As one of the directors of this firm, he is always happy to see the wife of a Very Important Person like Mike Mitchell.

"Do you have an appointment?" she asks.

I smile apologetically. "I'm sorry. I meant to call ahead, but then I—can I see him, anyway? Please tell him it's

Tamra Mitchell." I know he's in because I checked on the way over with a quick phone call.

She purses her lips. Finally, she asks me to take a seat. Minutes later I'm in John Moller's office, having brushed away the offer of refreshments.

"What can I do for you, Tamra?"

I've already apologized for dropping in like this, so I get straight to the point. "I don't know if Mike told you, but we have big plans. Mike's going to run for governor. Isn't it great?"

"Yes, I heard. Congratulations."

"Good. Well, those plans mean I'm taking a more proactive role in his career. I'll be acting as a kind of non-official adviser." I smile.

He smiles, too. Then, just as I knew he would, he replies, "Yes, yes! I did hear something about that."

"Good."

He raises an eyebrow, waiting for my question.

"I'd like to get a snapshot of our financial situation, so that I know what we can spare for the campaign."

Now he's raised two eyebrows. "I already forwarded that information to Mike. Do you have a specific question about that?"

My jaw almost drops, but I catch myself, just in time.

"He's so busy at the moment, it's hard to get anything out of him. That's why I'm here, I thought it would be faster to talk to you." I smile, cross my legs, bend down slightly to scratch my ankle, thereby giving him a peak of my peaks, so to speak. Then I remember that I'm old and discarded. "When did you give him the information, did you say?"

He sighs—just a tiny, low-nose sigh, but I catch it, anyway. He reaches out for the keyboard and types something. I lean forward to see the screen, but he gives me a look that makes me sit back. After a few keystrokes he says, "I emailed the financial reports last month."

"Okay, good, that's what I thought," I mumble. "So how much have we got? To spare I mean, for the campaign. Underwriting it. The campaign. Expenses."

"You want me to answer that right now? I'll need to pull up your files."

"Could you?"

"I would need time, to—"

"Just ballpark is fine for now."

Sigh. "Okay, so with the exposure from the loans you took out recently…"

"Exposure?"

"The financing of the loans."

"Ah, yes, okay. And what were those exactly?"

"The liquidation of some of your portfolio and the drawdown against the company assets."

"The company assets?" He must be wondering if there's an echo in here. I know I am.

"It's got your signature. Tamra. All of it. It's all in the reports. In the email."

Something comes to mind. It happened last year, I think. I was on the phone with his son Jack, and Mike shoved some document in front of me, handed me a pen, and tapped at the spot marked with some kind of sticker.

"What's this?" I mouthed, already poised to sign.

"Life insurance renewal." Then he tapped his watch and whispered, "I gotta go, baby doll."

I smiled at him and quickly signed the papers. He kissed me on the lips, and he was gone.

I can hear Joan's voice now, shrill and panicked. *I was*

signing whatever papers he put in front of me. I never asked because I just assumed he knew best.

I didn't sign because I assumed he knew best. I signed because he called me baby doll.

I lean forward and cross my arms on the desk. "Can you forward that to me, as well?"

There's just a sliver of hesitation, but he thinks better of it. With a few keystrokes, he has sent it on to me. I can't wait to get my hands on it.

I get up to leave.

"Wait, I almost forgot, can you forward me a copy of our prenup?" My hand is on the doorknob and I'm about to step outside when I ask, as if it was an afterthought.

"It's already in the email I'm forwarding," he says.

"It is?"

"Mike asked for a copy. Along with the other documents."

Chapter Seven

The first thing I do when I get home is check my email. True to his word, John Moller has forwarded the reports of our finances. I don't think he's told Mike of my visit—not yet anyway—otherwise, Mike would have called me to ask about that. But if he brings it up when he gets home, I'm ready to spin a tale of wanting to be a part of his new career.

"I can help with the campaign, you know I can. I can organize fundraisers and media interviewers for you. It's a chance to do something together." That's what I'll say, if it comes up. And that I wanted it to be a surprise. He'll like that.

But I can't make sense of the report. It's just lots of numbers and stocks and names of funds, but it does look a lot like he's been moving money around. But the worst thing, the short paragraph that makes my head spin and my stomach lurch as I read it, is at the end of the email.

As per your request, please find attached a copy of yours and Tamra's prenuptial agreement. When you're ready, let me know what amendments you require.

I don't take rejection well. Does anyone? I don't know. But I've had more than my share of it, and frankly stoicism is an overrated virtue. It's bad enough that he's making a fool of me with his floozy. It kills me that he doesn't love me anymore. Mike is the love of my life, and now he goes out of his way to make sure I end up with nothing? After everything I did for him? I saved his reputation. I saved his career. I saved his ass.

No way.

I already know what I'm going to do. I think I've always known, ever since I found those ridiculous panties, but now that I've actually made the decision, I just need the opportunity.

I'm sitting in our elegant living room, sipping on a glass of Bryant's Cab Sav as I ponder how to go about my new plan. I'm especially enjoying the wine. It's one of his favorite, and most expensive, and I haven't even decanted it. I wouldn't normally go through an entire bottle of wine by myself—heck, those days are long gone—so I have every intention of enjoying maybe just one more glass and pouring the rest down the sink. But then I hear the key in the lock and I realize he has come home early.

"Hey baby doll!" He kisses my hair, removes his coat, asks about my day.

"Oh, you know, shopping, this and that," I reply, breezily.

He smiles, then notices the bottle on the coffee table. "I'll join you, let me get myself a glass."

I'm gratified to find that John Moller hasn't called him about my visit. And why would he? My explanation was perfectly believable.

"Hey babe," Mike says now, returning with the glass in his hand, "I thought I'd take Maddie out to dinner tonight, would you mind?" Then he notices the wine label and raises an eyebrow, but he doesn't say anything, just pours more wine into my glass and then into his own.

"Without me, you mean?" I ask, but not unkindly.

He crinkles his face into an apology. "I just thought it would be nice for us to catch up, a father-daughter thing. But only if that's okay with you," he rushes to add.

"Sure, I don't mind, I get it," I say. "Where are you taking her?"

"Bin54," he says, smiling. Of course, it's her favorite restaurant. Although it hardly seems worth the trip. Judging by the looks of her, she'll probably nibble on a salad leaf and then declare she couldn't fit another thing in. But my heart quickens and I feel a rush of excitement, because Bin54 is maybe an hour from here, and they won't be back for hours.

It's perfect.

Thirty minutes later I stand on the porch and wave goodbye, like the good housewife and stepmother that I am, and the moment they're out of sight, I run to the back of the house where the garden tools are kept and grab a shovel. I'm shaking as I gather everything I need and finally I get into the car. I ask myself briefly if I really want to do this, then I drive off before I have time to talk myself out of it.

Chapter Eight

It takes me almost an hour to get to where she's buried. To where I buried her. Driving here, I thought I might panic at the last moment and change my mind, so I kept the memory of that flimsy thong at the forefront of my mind, along with the knowledge that he was a cheating, two-faced jerk who was about to dump me.

Using my iPhone for light, I look for the exact spot where I hid her. I left a marker, in a moment of guilt, actually. Little did I know then it would come in handy. I carved a cross on the tree above her grave that night, with a screwdriver I found in the trunk of the car. I rush from tree to tree, feeling the bark under my fingers. I'm never going to find it. This is ridiculous. I should go home. It's not too late. Then I spot it.

There's never anyone around at this time of night because it's too dark, and there are no houses in the vicinity. Lucky for me, it's been raining lately, which is going to make my task a little bit easier. I begin to dig and there's a moment when I wonder what I would do if she's not there, but she's not buried very deep, and it doesn't take too long to uncover her. I just need to do it enough so that she'll be found. I don't expose her face because I don't think I could bear it. I don't even know if she still has one. I just need a shoe, a foot, but when I get to her arm I suddenly realize she's in such bad shape it makes me gag. I look up at the sky and take in a deep breath to ward off the nausea. I can't be sick, not here. Then when I expose the flash of a red jacket, I figure it's enough.

There. Fuck you, Mike Mitchell.

After that I'm on autopilot. I drive home as fast I can without breaking the law and go straight to shower. I was going to pretend to be asleep when he came back. I thought I wouldn't sleep at all, after what I'd done, but it must have been the physical work that did it, because next thing I know it's morning and Mike is snoring softly beside me.

"I think I'll come home for lunch today," he says, knotting his tie in front of the mirror. "Maddie's only here for a week so we may as well make the most of it."

"That's sweet," I reply, trying to keep my voice level. I'm still in bed, propped up against the pillows, my thumbs flicking the screen of my phone seemingly absentmindedly. But I am vibrating with anticipation. I've been checking for news incessantly, although I don't really expect it would happen this fast. But Mike coming home for lunch feels like an extra bonus. I can't believe my luck.

After he's gone, I just stay in bed. I don't know what else to do. I check for news on my phone, then I reach for the magazine on my bedside table, flick through it without taking in any of it. I hear Sophia come in. She sings out to me like she always does. "Hello! Mrs. Mitchell!" I wonder if she'll do the same with the next Mrs. Mitchell. Mrs. Mitchell the Third. No of course not. There isn't going to be another Mrs. Mitchell.

I get up and dressed, then go downstairs to let her know that Mike is coming home for lunch.

"You've had good news, yes?" she says.

"What do you mean?"

She raises a hand to her own cheek and smiles. "You look happy."

Later, when we've finished eating, I imagine watching us through the window. We must look so normal, like an ordinary twenty-first century family, the three of us together in the same room doing completely separate things.

Madison has settled on the couch, her long legs stretched out so there's no room for anyone else, and now she's glued to her iPhone. I do all the right things, like this is a normal day, but inside I'm so tight I can barely breathe.

I clear the table, by myself (surprise!), and wonder what I'll do the rest of the day. My husband thinks he's leaving me for some ding-dong bubble-head that has more legs than sense. I don't know who she is yet. I've tried to check his phone, but I don't know his passwords and anyway, he uses his thumbprint to unlock it, but hey! Who cares! She can have him! And by the time I'm done with him, she won't be pleased. I'm nervous, but also excited. Like it's Christmas morning, or something.

What should I do with myself on this sunny afternoon, I wonder? Shopping, maybe? Get my hair done? Mike is checking stocks on his laptop, and I made sure the TV's on, even though it's some program no one's watching. If I could, I would have sent Madison away today, but she won't listen to anything I say.

I watch her from the corner of my eye, all angles and not an ounce of fat on her. Sophia, our housekeeper, cooked a peach cobbler for dessert because it used to be Madison's favorite, but Madison bluntly told her she didn't want any. I could see how hurt Sophia was, and after she got everything ready for lunch, I told her she could leave for the day. "Madison and I will clean up," I said. As if. Then after she left, I brought it up with Madison.

"I'm just not into that kind of food anymore, Tamra. It's not good for you. Too much sugar, too much fat, and you should think about laying off yourself, if you don't mind me saying."

I did mind, very much, because actually I'm in pretty good shape for my age. That's what hours of yoga and Pilates will do every week.

"You could have had some, just for Sophia's sake. Or at least pretend to look forward to it. She went to all that trouble."

"But that's what we pay her for, isn't it?"

When did she get so cynical? She'd better watch herself, or she'll end up like me. Bitter and twisted. I'm about to tell her exactly that but something on the TV catches her eye. I follow her gaze.

"… on the edge of Uwharrie National Forest near Badin Lake. The body was found early this morning by a group of hikers. Jennifer Alton is on the scene."

"Oh, my God!" Madison shrieks, her hand flying to her mouth.

"Jesus, Maddie!" Mike jumps. We're all startled. I didn't know my heart could beat so fast.

She points at the TV. "Dad! That's just up from our

house!" She's right of course, except it's no longer our house.

"Yes, Brian, as you can see behind me, the police are still working the area where the remains of the body were found, not far from a popular walking track. At this stage we don't know exactly how long the body was there for. We can say that the woman has been buried here for at least one year, probably longer. The cause of death has not been identified, but it's highly likely it will be ruled as a homicide."

I'm frozen. I know in my heart that this is the moment where everything changes. Where we have crossed a line onto the other side, and I don't know what is going to happen next.

"Can you see, Dad? It's the dock in the back—"

"I'm not blind, Maddie!" he says.

I can't take my eyes off him, looking for signs of shock, distress, anything that shows he's still human, and while he is frowning, he looks more vaguely curious than frightened.

Wow, you're good. I think.

Chapter Nine

Last night I decided, in the privacy of my own mind, that I would henceforth refer to the mystery owner of that thong as *The Slut*. Whenever Mike's cell phone chimes, buzzes, or rings, I wonder if it's her, The Slut. If she is so brazen as to call him at home. And it's ringing now but he doesn't hear it because he's in the shower, so I reach across his side of the bed and snatch it from the side table.

"Mike Mitchell's phone, this is *Mrs.* Mitchell," I say, honey rolling off my tongue.

"Mrs. Mitchell, this is detective Torres of Charlotte-Mecklenburg, is your husband at home?"

Now I wish I hadn't answered. I sit up, propping myself against the pillows. "Yes, but he can't come to the phone right this minute."

"That's all right, Ma'am, we'd like to come by and talk to him, informally."

"Can I ask what it's about?"

"We'd rather talk to him, Mrs. Mitchell. Can you tell him we'll come by in an hour?"

The door of the bathroom opens. Mike is rubbing a towel over his hair, and it takes him a moment to register that I'm holding his phone.

He mouths, 'Who is it?'

I hold up an index finger. "All right."

"Thank you, Mrs. Mitchell."

When I tell him the cops are coming to talk to him, he asks me what it's about.

"They didn't say." I can't look at him. I get out of bed and head straight for the shower.

There are two of them. Detective Torres and Detective O'Brien. I expected suspicion to be etched onto their faces, but no. In fact, they're surprisingly friendly. We're in the smaller sitting room because there's no wall between the main one and the entrance hall, and I don't want Madison to show up in the middle of our 'informal chat' when she wakes up.

Once we get through the preliminaries (thank you for your time, we appreciate your cooperation in this matter), Torres says, "Mr. Mitchell, and Mrs. Mitchell, yesterday morning, skeletal remains were found by a group of hikers near the Uwharrie Forest."

Skeletal remains? Surely that's a bit of an exaggeration. Maybe that's just cop speak.

"Yes," Mike says, a hint of caution in his tone. Me, my hands are shaking. I press them together between my thighs, as if I'm cold.

"We've identified the young woman as Charlene Donovan."

It's like a punch in the gut, hearing her name. My heart

pounds in my ears. I turn to look at Mike, and he has turned white. He keeps shaking his head, like it's a mistake.

They don't say anything for a few seconds, then O'Brien asks, "Does the name ring a bell?"

"Yes," he says, with just a hint of a stutter. "I believe so, she worked in my office for a short time, isn't that right, Tamra?"

I didn't expect the question, but I recognize the deflection.

"I—I think so," I reply.

"Did you know Charlene Donovan, Mrs. Mitchell?"

"Me? Not very well. I might've met her at a function or something."

"You don't remember?"

"Not really."

Mike does a good job pretending to be relaxed. He stretches an arm out along the back of the armchair, crosses and re-crosses his legs, and I almost want to sneak over to him and whisper in his ear: *just stop, you're making it worse*.

Almost.

But he's so pale, I feel for him. And tense. Which means he bites the inside of his mouth.

"Just so we're clear, she was working for you, correct?" O'Brien asks.

"Not exactly. She was an intern in my company. And I didn't employ her. We have HR for that. I don't get involved in the hiring and firing of staff."

"I wasn't suggesting you'd hired her yourself, just that she had worked in your office."

"As an employee, yes." Mike points out, as if clarification was needed. If that's the way he's going to handle this chat, we're going to be here a while.

"And that was two years ago, for a few weeks, over summer," he adds.

If that had been me, I would have at least pretended to care. I would have said it's really, really sad, poor girl, so young, and that sort of thing. I would have asked if her parents had been notified, and if there was anything I could do to help. God. Who am I kidding? I'm just the same. I try to summon up even a modicum of sadness for her, but I can't. What does it say about me? That I'm as selfish as he is, I guess. Maybe we are meant for each other, after all. Or maybe the grief for her will come later. Maybe I'll wake up one day soon, and I will put my head in my hands and cry for her.

But not today.

"Here's the thing that we're having difficulties with, Mr. Mitchell," Torres says, leaning forward and resting his elbows on his knees. "We believed, until two days ago, that Charlene returned to Austin, over there in the fine state of Texas—"

"I know where Austin is, detective," Mike says, rudely I think, but Torres doesn't seem to notice. He resumes as if it was a perfectly legitimate interruption.

"Of course." He says. "So we know she went back there right after she finished her stint with your office."

Mike nods quickly.

"That's why we never looked for her over this way, you see?"

Mike nods, he sees.

"Weeks before she finished the internship, she purchased a ticket for her flight home. Airline records show that she took the flight. That was…" He licks his index finger, then flicks through pages of a small notebook.

51

"Twenty-third of November, two years ago," O'Brien says.

Torres shoots her a look.

"Yeah. Right. Twenty-third of November. For various reasons I won't go into, we know she was there, back in Austin on that day, and that was the last time anyone's seen her, or heard from her. So you see why we're confused, Mr. Mitchell."

Mike does a quick shake of the head. "No. I have no idea why you're confused."

Torres cocks his head just a little, his frown deepening. "Because she shows up back our way, when all this time our colleagues have been looking for her in Texas."

"But what do you want me to do about it?"

"She must have come back for a reason. Do you know what that might be?"

"Why would I know? I'm not a mind-reader, I had nothing to do with this woman beyond her very short employment in my office."

He probably doesn't mean to sound as defensive as that, but it's too late, and O'Brien quietly raises an eyebrow.

"Did you know she had come back?" she asks.

"No."

"What about you, Mrs. Mitchell?"

"Me? N—no!"

"Is there anything you can tell us?" O'Brien asks, her gaze going from Mike to me, and back again. We both shake our heads, and Mike even puts a finger on his lips, in a show of at least thinking about it.

"Well, then, I think we're done here, what do you say, O'Brien?" Torres says, pushing his hands against his thighs as he stands.

She nods, but not so enthusiastically, I notice. She may not think they're done quite yet, but she'll go with it for now. Torres even apologizes for the intrusion. Some people are like that around money. Mike pats him on the back and thanks him for doing his job, his face awash with relief.

We've only just shut the door after them when Mike announces he has to go to his office. He can't wait to get out of the house more likely, so that we don't have to talk about what just happened. That's fine with me, better than fine. Although I wish he would stick around until Her Royal Highness Madison gets out of bed so he can tell her about the cops paying us a visit, and why. She probably wouldn't even care, but still, I think that's his job.

It's time for phase two. I retreat to the kitchen and make the call. It doesn't take long. I tell the receptionist that I have information regarding Charlene Donovan, she takes down my details and says someone will get back to me right away.

"I trust they'll be discrete," I say, "in case I can't take the call right there and then."

"Don't worry. That's our job," she replies.

While I wait, I pour over any mention of Charlene online. I'm so absorbed that I don't hear Madison coming in. What alerts me to her presence is the kettle being filled.

"Hey, how did you sleep?"

"Okay," she says. She grabs a lemon and pops it onto the electric juicer, then pours the juice in a mug, followed by hot water. The whole thing takes a couple of minutes during which she doesn't even look my way.

"You want some honey with that?" I ask, getting off the stool. I meant it as a joke, but now she just looks at me, up and down, silently, as if to make some kind of point I guess, then goes back to her task.

"I'm going to the store shortly," I tell her. "Do you want to write me a list of stuff you'd like?" My phone pings with a text. "Just leave it on the counter. I have to take this call." And I walk out.

Chapter Ten

I push the shopping cart around, smiling at no one in particular, and take great care when picking up various items from Madison's list. I'm pleased to see there are things other than just celery on it. Things like tofu chips and almond milk. I could have just given it to Sophia, of course, but I still feel badly about how dismissive Madison had been toward her.

I see my neighbor Alice way up the other end of the aisle. That's good I think, as I wave and smile in her direction. Alice confessed to me once that her husband, a retired police officer, was depressed. I offered to help, suggested some community meetings he could go to, and since then she's avoided me.

I do a little wave at a young woman standing near the cheeses, just because she looks like someone I used to know. That's how unhinged I am today. She frowns at me in confusion, but I don't let that stop me. If I keep telling myself that everything is normal, and this is a very ordinary day, maybe I'll believe it.

It dawns on me she reminds me of Patti. I owe her one,

and I have to say, she surprised me. I wouldn't have picked her for a card-carrying member of the sisterhood. But all Mike said that night was, "I heard you came by to take me out to lunch." He gave me that curly smile of his, and I replied, "That's right darling. What can I say? I just missed you."

When I get to the checkout, I notice a woman talking into her phone on the other side. She's turned slightly away from me. I put everything onto the moving belt and steal glances in her direction. She puts her phone away and looks right at me. My heart quickens. I've never met her, and yet I know exactly who this is, and I do my best to look away.

Outside, I'm loading the groceries into the trunk of my car when my cell rings. It makes me jump, but it's Lauren.

"Hi, Lauren. What's up?" I look around to see where the woman has gone, but I can't see her. I shake my head, tell myself to act natural. Maybe I was mistaken.

"Sorry, Lauren, what did you say?"

"I said I've been dying to know, have you spoken to him yet?"

I sigh, close the trunk, and lean against the side of the car. Lauren really needs to stop bugging me about this because it's getting annoying. "I told you already. I have plans to make."

"I know, but I figured it must be impossible to be in the same house with him, or even in the same room. Did you talk to him when you got home? Like I told you to?"

"Firstly, you don't get to tell me when or how to talk to him—"

"Oh, don't be so snippy."

"—and secondly, that was our first dinner with

Madison around. I was hardly going to spring it on him then, was I."

"You're just making excuses."

"No, I'm not. I barely see him and when I do, Madison's with us. He decided to take her out for dinner the night before last. To catch up properly, apparently."

"Really? Wow, in your shoes, I don't think I could have gone."

I feel my mouth twitch, just a tiny bit. "Well, I didn't. He wanted it to be a father-daughter thing. He did ask if I minded," I quickly add.

"You didn't?"

"No, I get it, that's cool."

"So what did you do?"

"Nothing, I stayed home, watched something, went to bed."

I can hear her take a drag of a cigarette. Lauren is an occasional smoker, very occasional. I used to smoke before I met Mike. Just thinking about it gives me a pang of nostalgia for those clubbing, drug-induced, hazy days. Right now, I would kill for a cigarette.

"The night before last? That's funny. I came by your house that night to check in on you. There was no one home."

I screw my eyes shut. "I—I went to bed early. Did you try to call me?"

Another drag. I can almost smell the smoke. "Uh huh, it went straight to voicemail."

There's movement in my peripheral vision. I turn to look. It's the woman from earlier. She's walking straight over to me as I hear Lauren ask if I'm still there. The woman stops just three feet from me. She puts out her

57

hand, and for a moment, I think I'm supposed to shake it. But then I notice the small white business card.

"I'll call you back," I tell Lauren and hang up.

"Fiona Martin, from the Tribune. Here." She shoves the business card at me.

I take it, recoiling a little.

"Are you aware that your husband had an affair with Charlene Donovan?"

"Excuse me?"

"Charlene Donovan, her body was found yesterday morn—"

"Yes, I know. What does that have to do with my husband?"

I look around. Is anyone watching us?

"She worked for him. She did an internship in his department. The summer before she went missing."

I wince. "So what? What does that prove?"

"They had an affair, did you know that? He forced her to have an abortion."

"What?"

"Did you know?" she says again, cocking her head at me.

"Who told you that?"

"I can't tell you."

"This is ridiculous," I stammer. I look around again, scan the parking lot to see if anyone has heard, but there aren't many people around. Then I see Alice. She's unlocking her car. Without warning, Fiona Martin takes it up a notch. "I'm with the Tribune. We're running a story on your husband's affair and the abortion. Do you want to comment, Mrs. Mitchell?"

She's so loud. Alice's head turns to look at us. I try to

smile, but my lips are trembling, and I can't. She raises an eyebrow, and I shake my head.

"How did you know who I am? Have you been following me?" I almost shriek.

"Do you want to comment?"

"Of course, I don't want to comment! I have nothing to say to you." I turn away, about to open the car door but I'm shaking so much that I drop the keys. She bends down faster than I and picks them up for me.

"We're running the story, Mrs. Mitchell. It's well and truly in the public interest, and not just because that means your husband is bound to be a person of interest in the disappearance of Charlene Donovan—"

Alice is outright staring now. And she's no longer alone. I snap my head around to Fiona Martin. "What did you say?"

"—but your husband is planning to run for governor, and considering he makes no secret of being *pro-life*," she makes sarcastic air-quotes with two fingers, "people should know who they're dealing with. Wouldn't you agree?"

"Is everything all right?" I turn to see Alice, worry etched on her face. She looks at me, then at Fiona.

"Yes, everything's fine," I tell her. Fiona opens her mouth to say something, but I shoot her a look and put my hand on Alice's arm. "Really, thank you, I've got this. I'll talk to you later."

She hesitates, just for a second. "If you're sure," she says finally, and turns around, reluctantly, looking back as she returns to her friend.

I'm pressing the button on the key to unlock the car but I'm doing it wrong and it's too fast and it's going *click, click* as the locks move up and down behind the glass.

"If you have anything to say, Mrs. Mitchell, you need to do it today, now."

Finally, I get it right, and I slide into the driver seat and pull the door, but she's holding on. I pull harder and she lets go. At last I have the key in the ignition and start the car.

"She was twenty years old, Mrs. Mitchell."

She had to shout that last part because the windows are up. I look at her. She's leaning forward, one hand against the window.

"What?"

"When she was murdered."

"Go away!" I yell. She steps back just as I accelerate out of there.

Chapter Eleven

That little exercise in the supermarket was her idea.

"We get a couple of people to see me blindsiding you. Make sure you're trying to get away from me. Nothing like a little humiliation to distract people from even suspecting you're my source."

"Fuck, you're good," I said.

I wasn't sure what to make of her at first. I had left a message at the Tribune because Mike hates that paper— Lord knows why, something to do with them being a bunch of 'left wingers,' but I expected a man to call me back. One of the guys who gets the bylines on the political stories. Instead, Fiona Martin called. I told her everything about Mike's affair with Charlene. No, not everything. That would be too much too soon. But more than enough to get her interested, and definitely enough to cause Mike some serious pain.

I thought I'd be relieved now that this part is done, but I'm shaking so much that I have to stop the car after a couple of blocks. I close my eyes and slowly release my grip on the steering wheel. My heart is thumping in my chest.

I reach for the phone and call Mike. Surprisingly, he answers on the first ring.

"Some journalist just accosted me, Fiona—"

He cuts me off. "I know. She called me, too, an hour ago."

"She's going to write about the abortion."

"Yeah! I don't think so. I told her what to do with her filthy lies and innuendos."

That makes me take a sharp breath. Filthy lies and innuendos? That's stretching it somewhat, I think. Is he forgetting who he's talking to?

"I told them if they print a word of this, they'll find themselves in court. Assholes," he goes on.

"Do you think they'll hold off?"

"They better."

"She said just now that they're running the story. Tomorrow, I think."

"Fuck them, they shouldn't harass you. How dare they?" he yells.

I pull the phone away from my ear. "Where are you?"

He sighs. "In the office."

"Maybe you should come down. If there are people around…"

"Yeah, I know, but that fucking bitch—"

"Mike, stop!"

There's a pause, and in my mind I can see him taking a hold of himself. He would be swinging his head left and right, stretching his neck. It might even make a snapping noise. Like a fighter getting ready. I used to find that sexy, once upon a time. Now it makes my stomach lurch.

"What should we do?" I ask, my voice small and frightened.

"Nothing. Leave it. I'll take care of it."

"If you say so. Will you be home later?"

"Of course. We can talk then."

"Okay." Then just before he hangs up, "Mike?"

"Yes?"

I picture him with the phone tight against his ear. Sweat beading just under his nose. "How did she find out?"

"How the fuck should I know?"

In my memory of that night, the night that Mike killed her, everything is hyperreal. The leaves and trees illuminated by the car's headlights are so green as to be almost fluorescent. It was late summer, so still too early for that almost kaleidoscopic foliage, those vivid shades of reds, ochres and golds that North Carolina is famous for, and that we enjoy even in those foothills.

I don't like to remember, obviously. But that doesn't mean that I forgot. First there was the affair, then the payout and the abortion, and that was supposed to be the end of it.

Except I saw them. I saw her get into his car when he wasn't even supposed to be there. I followed them, from a distance. What else was I supposed to do? First it was a mile, then another. I understood, finally, that they had tricked me. That they were running away together.

I kept following them, not knowing why or what I would do when they arrived at their destination, but I kept up with them. We drove like that for maybe half an hour, until we came to the edge of the forest. They turned off the well-lit avenues, into the darker roads. I had to switch off my headlights and put more distance between us, or else they'd see me. That's how dark it was.

We weren't far from Badin Lake by then, so I figured that they must be going to our old house, but I couldn't understand why. We'd already sold the house at that point, but the paperwork had only just exchanged hands and it was sitting empty. Off for another tryst maybe? In somebody else's empty house? Just for kicks?

Then out of the blue the passenger door opened. The car was still moving, and it lurched to an abrupt stop. For a moment I thought they'd seen me, and my heart skipped a beat. I had nowhere to go. I quickly stopped and turned off the motor, blood pounding in my ears, and in the distance, I watched Charlene get out of the car. The light came on inside and I saw Mike in profile through the darkened rear window. He was wearing that Panthers cap. The cap that was always in the back of the car somewhere. It's not there anymore, I threw it away. I couldn't bear the sight of it.

Charlene disappeared into the woods and the car sat there, idling, the headlights illuminating the rain that had begun to fall. I thought he'd never move, but it was probably only ten or fifteen minutes before he took off again. I didn't want to turn on the engine yet because it was so quiet. I was worried Charlene would hear me out there, so I waited. Then, just as I was about to turn the ignition, I saw her. She had run back into the road and stopped like a deer in the headlights, and Mike just drove right into her. It was so fast, so brutal, almost as if he'd accelerated when he saw her. I watched her body bounce on impact and in my mind's eye, it's as if she was flying. But I know she wasn't. It all happened in the space of a second. My hand flew to my mouth and I stifled the scream that roared in my throat so hard it hurt. The car sat there, the rain fell some more, and when his door opened I reversed out of there as fast as I possibly could.

I reach for Fiona Martin's crumpled card that has fallen on my lap, and that's when I notice there's something scribbled on the back of it.

"Joe's Bar & Grill, Jamestown, 1 hour" it says. Then below that, she's added "call me if you can't make it."

I can make it. It's a twenty-minute drive but that's fine with me. I don't know anyone who lives around there so I'm less likely to run into someone I know.

"I talked to my boss," she says, by way of introduction. "We're running with it, but I need more specifics. Dates, names, places. Also, you said earlier that he convinced her to have an abortion. Can you clarify what you mean by 'convinced'?"

"He offered her money." I'm about to say more but the waitress has arrived with our coffees. We wait silently until she leaves.

"Blackmail money?" she blurts out. I can see how excited she is by all this. I can't tell if it's the cloak and dagger angle, or if she really thinks it's a great story.

I shrug. "I guess you could call it that. We had to sell our second house to pay her out, so yeah, I guess that would qualify as blackmail money." We didn't pay her out in the end, because she was dead, and dead people don't need money. But I'm not ready to tell Fiona Martin that.

She makes a low whistle and scribbles furiously. "And then she went back to Austin?"

I nod. "We paid for her ticket too, believe it or not."

After a few minutes of scribbling, she puts her pen down and sits back. "Why are you telling me all this?" she asks.

"I thought you would have figured that out. Revenge, of course."

"For what?"

"That's my business."

She cocks her head at me. "You must hate your husband very much."

I flinch. "Quite the opposite, in fact, but let's say that I have my reasons."

She makes a note. I crane my neck to see what it says. *Hell hath no fury like a woman scorned*, probably. Funny, but Mike taught me that quote, in jest of course. Little did he know. Fiona catches my eye and closes her notebook.

"I looked you up on the Tribune's website, by the way, you haven't written up much lately, not like you used to. Why is that?"

She shrugs. "That's my business."

I laugh, in spite of myself. "Touché," I say. But she's all work and no play and doesn't even smile. She pushes her notepad across the table and hands me her pen.

"Can you write the address of the clinic? And the exact date, I still need to confirm."

"Yeah, there's a bit of a problem," I say, writing it all down.

She raises an eyebrow. "What problem?"

"The doctor, who was going to… who performed the surgery. He's incredibly discreet. So discreet, in fact, that he keeps no records whatsoever. Or those were the exact words that were told to me at the time. But I believe it."

She looks incredulous. "You're saying there's no proof at all?"

"Had there been, I would have left an anonymous tip."

"I'm not touching this."

I chuckle. "It's a bit late now, you just announced it all in the parking lot of Best—"

"That was a mistake," she snaps, leaning down to pick up her purse.

I reach across and put a hand on her arm. "Wait. There was an exchange of funds. The clinic, they got paid. I could check at my end, go through his bank account, can you crosscheck with the clinic's bank?"

She stops, waits, then she says, "I don't know. Maybe." She chews her bottom lip. "You're going to tell me all this again, and I'm going to video you, okay?"

I scoff. "You must be joking."

She puts a hand up, palm out. "I won't use it, but I have to show my boss where my information comes from. No one will ever know you told me. You have my word. But I'm not going to get sued just because you want to indulge in a spot of revenge."

I try to argue, but there's no point. It's that or nothing. We leave and she records me in her car. It's harder to tell my tale with an iPhone pointed at me, but she prompts with all the right questions and we get it done. Still. By the time I get home, I feel the weight of anxiety in my stomach.

When Mike walks in after his day at work, it's as if nothing happened. He's completely relaxed and he and Madison immediately settle themselves in the living room, and within minutes they're crapping on about the merits of offshore outsourcing in a global age. I mentally shoot daggers at him. I am calling him every name under the sun, silently. It must have worked because he finally notices me, leaning against the doorjamb.

"Do you have a minute? I could use your help in the kitchen." I mean it as a joke because I want to keep things light-hearted for Madison's sake. I mean, it's obviously a joke, since I don't spend that much time in there. Just on the days that Sophia isn't here. But I guess the 1950s are still well and truly with us, because neither of them react. Instead, he dislodges his arm from her shoulders while Madison frowns at me.

"Sorry princess," he says. "Hold that thought."

Madison shoots me a look that speaks volumes of her disapproval before running back upstairs, and I lead Mike into the smaller sitting room at the front. The one we never used until recently. Now we seem to live in it.

"You seem to be very relaxed." I look into his face. "Shouldn't you be worried?"

"Of course I'm worried!" he snaps. "I've called Alex Pace, and he's onto it. Cease and desist." He runs a hand through his hair. "I don't know if that's enough, I'm waiting to hear back."

He is anxious. I see that now. No, it's more than that, he's terrified. It brings an unexpected jolt of pleasure to me.

"Fuck them. I'll sue them. That fucking bitch!"

"Keep your voice down! We need to figure out who told her, don't you see? Do you have any ideas?"

"Don't you think I've been racking my brain? I have enemies! It's called politics!"

I almost laugh. He hasn't even officially announced his

candidature yet. "It's not that, surely. It's more personal than that," I say.

He flashes me a look, somewhere between anger and loathing. Suddenly I feel so alone in this house, surrounded by people who hate me.

"I thought it was only Pastor Frank and the doctor at the clinic that knew about the abortion," I say. "Was there anyone else?"

"Other than you, you mean?"

I stare into his face, trying to gauge whether he really believes that. "Because I really want my name plastered on the front page in connection to that... episode. Is that what you think?"

He turns away from me. We're both silent, lost in our own thoughts. I pretend to rack my brain. "So there's Pastor Frank," I resume, "and—"

He scoffs sharply. "You can't possibly suggest that he would have been the one—"

"To tell the papers? How would I know? I'm just going through the list of people who definitely knew about the abortion."

He winces at the word, the sight of which also brings me a rush of pleasure. I resolve to say it a lot.

"There's the doctor at the abortion clinic, obviously," I continue.

"He was paid handsomely."

"Maybe his costs went up."

"He would have approached us first, surely."

Us? Wow, that's something else. Suddenly we're a couple, a team. *Us* vs them. This from the man who comes home with sexy lingerie in his back pocket.

"Sophia?"

"You must be joking," he scoffs, then catches himself. "Unless you told her?"

"Hardly."

"That's it, then."

"What about Patti? Does she know?" I ask.

"No. Of course not."

But there's a sliver of hesitation, then a determination in his face that does not ring true. I think he's lying. I think Patti did know, about the whole sordid affair and its sordid conclusion. That makes sense. That would be why she didn't snitch on me the other day. She knows it's probably true. What about the new one, Miss. Victoria's Secret, does she know? I wonder. "Fiona Martin knows about you running for governor," I say.

He bites at the side of his thumb. It's funny, it's the kind of thing Madison would do.

"I mean, it's not top secret, obviously," I continue. "We talked about it with Rob and Bethany—"

He closes his eyes briefly.

"—but it does make you wonder."

He turns to me. "Wonder what?"

I shrug. "She must have been making calls. She must have asked around, about you. She'd have to, right? They have to get their facts right, do their research…" I know she's done no such thing, yet, I just like seeing him squirm.

"It doesn't matter. Pace will take care of it."

He sure doesn't look like it doesn't matter. I almost feel regretful.

Almost.

"I think I'll go and make some calls," he says, rubbing a hand across his face. "Don't tell Maddie about all this, okay?" he adds.

"I won't. But speaking of Madison…"

"What?"

"How does she seem to you?"

"What do you mean? This has nothing—"

"No! God! I know that, I mean, don't you think she's really thin?"

"Maddie? No, not really." He frowns at me, impatient.

"She's lost weight since we last saw her. She's not eating much."

"Okay! So what? She's a young woman. She's taking care of herself. Good for her. What's wrong with that?"

"I don't think she's taking care of herself. Just look at her. Look at her hair!" I blurt out. He stares at me like I've got two heads.

"I really don't have time for this, Tamra. Not now, okay?" He retreats to his study and I sit here a while longer. Why is it I'm the only one who can see that there's something wrong with Madison?

Madison has long blond hair, with chemical highlights, that she flicks away from her face constantly, especially if she's nervous. She's like all those twenty-something women around here. A collection of Barbies. But heck, who am I to judge? I have long blond hair with chemical highlights that I flick away from my face every five minutes.

But now her hair is listless. It's lost its sheen, and Madison is very conscious of her good looks. Too much, sometimes. Which, coming from me, is saying something. She used to have a small mole on her right cheekbone. The size of a freckle. She hated it. I told her about Cindy Crawford, supermodel extraordinaire. "She had a mole on her lip. It became her trademark, almost. It made her stand out." When she came back to us the following summer, it was gone.

So much for my 'love thyself' pep talks.

Chapter Twelve

EXCLUSIVE: North Carolina Self-Proclaimed Family Man and Political Hopeful had Links to Charlene Donovan.

By Fiona Martin

You may not have heard of the man who is at the center of this story, but that's about to change. Meet Mike Mitchell: self-made billionaire, fifty-two-year-old father of three, investment guru. Unless you're cashed up and looking for some solid returns with one of the most profitable boutique investment firms in this state, Mike Mitchell will mean nothing to you. But this successful businessman allegedly had an affair with a young woman whose body was found two days ago near Uwharrie National Forest.

Some people may question why Mike Mitchell's private life is in the public interest? There are a couple answers to that: The first one is that two years ago, Charlene Donovan completed an internship in Mike Mitchell's office. Then she disappeared. The investigation was concentrated in Austin, Texas, where Charlene Donovan resided, and was understood to have returned. The Tribune does not suggest that Mr. Mitchell is in any way involved with the disappearance of Ms. Donovan, but that doesn't mean he doesn't have a case to answer. What makes Mike Mitchell's role in the case particularly relevant, is that not only did he have an affair with Charlene, but she fell pregnant and Mike Mitchell allegedly insisted, and then arranged, for her to have an abortion. The police did not have this information when they searched for Charlene and Mike Mitchell was never questioned in relation to her disappearance.

The other thing you need to know about Mike Mitchell is that he is planning to run for the office of governor on a platform of family values and conservative principles. It's one thing to engage in an extramarital affair while pushing strong family values from the political pulpit, but quite another to coerce your mistress into having an abortion. We understand the principles of social conservatism touted by Mike Mitchell do not include advocating adultery or pregnancy terminations.

It's still dark when I wake up, but I see the glow of his phone first, then I realize he's awake, sitting up against the headboard. But it's his breathing that woke me up. He's like a caged animal, his nostrils dilating.

I put my hand on his arm. "Hey, how bad is it?"

When he turns to me, and I take in his face—the dark rings under his eyes that tell of a sleepless night, the paleness of his cheeks—I figure it's pretty bad.

But later, for the sake of Madison, he pulls himself together and I have to say, I'm a little impressed.

She's beyond upset. She's shaking and crying, and I

want to take her into my arms and console her, but hey, I'd have more luck getting that sort of trust from a turnip.

"Shh… it's all right, sweetheart," Mike whispers into her hair. He looks at me with a pained expression and does little shakes of the head. He doesn't know what to do. I put a tentative hand on her back, and she shrugs it off without looking up.

"It's all lies sweetheart, you understand? It's politics darling," he says. Then he looks at me with an apologetic smile and I understand that I'm not wanted, thanks very much. There's nothing I can possibly do down here, so I leave them to their sweet nothings and rush back upstairs.

Twenty minutes later I'm sitting on the end of the bed checking under my nails when he joins me.

"How is she?" I ask sweetly, matching his expression. What I want to ask is, *has she grown up yet? Because she's taking her sweet good time. Does she know the world does not revolve around her? No? I didn't think so.*

He sits next to me and runs a hand over his face. "She's lying down. She's scared, she thinks something is going to happen to me. It's not easy for her," he says, and I wait for him to give that little worried smile and say, *just like it's not easy for you, baby doll.* But waiting is all I do.

"You need to come clean, Mike."

He jolts. "What do you mean?"

"She's dead! This has gone beyond your reputation, wouldn't you say?"

He jumps off the bed, like his ass is on fire. "Are you out of your fucking mind?"

"Listen! Listen to me! Maybe it's related, have you thought of that?"

He stares at me like I'm speaking in tongues. "Related how?"

"I don't know! Maybe she killed herself! Maybe she ran away and fell with the wrong crowd? Shouldn't we tell the cops that we gave her all that money? Maybe that's a motive for someone, I don't know, or at least they could check if she—"

Suddenly his face is inches from mine. He jabs an index finger in my direction, over and over. "If you tell anyone about that, I swear to God—"

"Jesus, Mike. Relax, I'm just pointing out that things are not as simple as we thought, okay? I mean, I didn't know she was dead, did you?"

He stumbles backwards, his jaw slack. I'm enjoying myself way more than I expected. This is going to be fun.

"Well, did you?" I ask again. I can't help it. It's like picking at a scab.

"Jesus, Tamra! Of course not! How would I know that? Last I heard she got on that plane and that was that! You know that! What are you trying to say?"

Yeah, I didn't think he would, confess that is. But I have to give it to him, he's a good liar.

"Well, obviously, she came back. Which is odd when you think about it. She had a half a million bucks in her bank account, why wouldn't she take a vacation on an island somewhere? I know I would." I look at my nails when I say that, but I'm attuned to his every vibration. I know we never paid her, in the end. I just want to see if he twitches.

But he's had enough of my insinuations, he says, and thanks me *so* much for having his back before snatching his jacket from the back of the chair and storming off. First, he slams our bedroom door shut, and minutes later I hear the front door slam. I get up with a sigh and walk across the hall to Madison's room.

She's lying on her bed, both thumbs flicking up and down on the screen of her iPhone.

"You're okay?" I ask.

She frowns at the screen and without looking at me she says, "Where did Dad go?"

"He went for a walk. To clear his head."

I take a look around her bedroom. I rarely come in here. I don't feel welcome, and contrary to what Madison might believe, I respect her boundaries. So it's a strange feeling. Here I am, standing in my own house and yet my surroundings are surprisingly unfamiliar. Jack and Zach also had bedrooms, back in the day when they needed their own space here—when they were still kids, basically. Now they're just guest bedrooms, generic. They don't need their teddy bears enshrined in these walls.

Not Madison. She needs her own, special bedroom, and she has it. And it's very pretty, all girly pastels and gold. It's a corner bedroom and the two tall windows let plenty of light in. Her walls are peppered with framed self-affirmations in various cursive fonts. *Be bright, be happy; Never forget how talented you are; Love, love, love; This girl is not throwing away her shot; There are so many beautiful reasons to be happy; You got this; I LOVE ME.*

Everywhere you look feels like being trapped in a self-help workshop run by a demented sign-writer. I sure never had a bedroom like that. Maybe that's why I'm bitter and twisted.

"What did you say to him?" she asks, thumbs flicking.

"What makes you think I said anything?"

"Because he popped his head in here and said he had to get away from you for a few minutes." She looks up at me now.

She is so pale and drawn that I get a little stab of guilt.

I sit on the corner of the bed, just the teeniest little corner, only as much as would hold me so I don't fall off, but still she makes a show of moving away from me, like I'm in her space.

"You don't need to be so upset about the article. If anything, I'm the one who should be upset."

"You don't think I should be upset, when all these filthy lies and insinuations are being said about my dad?" she snorts with derision, and I wonder why she feels the need to parrot her father.

"It'll be okay, you'll see. It'll blow over."

She snorts again. "How would you know?"

If I had thought it through, instead of acting on impulse as per usual, I might have waited until after Madison had gone back before spilling the beans to Fiona Martin. She wouldn't have been so affected over there in Nexw York. And she'd have her mother close by.

And I wouldn't have to put up with the attitude.

But then again, I didn't have any time to lose. He was about to walk out on me.

Sorry, but that trumps Madison's feelings.

Chapter Thirteen

Jack called. He lives in LA. He studied architecture at Berkley and later he and a classmate formed their own firm over there. He's single, or so he says, but I secretly believe that he is gay and he doesn't want his father to know. Of Mike's three children, Jack is the one I get along with the most. His other son, Zach, is a film director, and he's based in New York, but currently, he's in London, working on a feature. I don't think he's that close to the family, and he hasn't called. Yet.

Jack has read the article online, and Mike spun his tale that this was the work of his detractors, as he now calls them. But the paper was going to publish a retraction and an apology, he said, tomorrow. Mike's lawyer had just confirmed it, so there was nothing to worry about.

I heard all that from just outside the door of his office, and I couldn't believe my ears. And the fact that he hadn't bothered to tell me any of this. Like I don't count. And maybe I don't, not anymore, because after our argument yesterday, he didn't come home until late and I knew he'd been with *her*. I pretended to be asleep when he slid into the bed. I wanted him to touch me, to spoon me the way we did sometimes, but he didn't. He just lay there like a piece of driftwood and no doubt stared at the ceiling while my eyes became hot with tears and I scrunched them up to stop myself from crying. It was all I could do not to turn around and put my hand on his soft chest. Or punch his face.

I imagined the two of them, limbs intertwined in between satin sheets. What did she say? I wondered. She saw the article, I know that because when it was barely dawn, and he was crying out in his sleep beside me, I got up and went through his pockets and bingo! Jesus, Mike! Can't you at least *try* to be discreet?

Thinking of you. Just remember. I've got your back. Love you

Was he on his knees, swearing that he had done nothing wrong, just like he did with me two years ago? Did she believe him? Of course, she did. He was getting a retraction, for fuck's sake. You had to admire the nerve of the guy. How long could he keep this up?

I shudder. *Forever…* says my paranoid brain. I took that note, crumpled the pale yellow paper into a ball and hid it in the back of a drawer. But there's something about it that tugs at my brain. It's the handwriting, I think. Something that feels, dare I say, familiar?

These are the thoughts twirling in my head as I stand here outside the door of his study, rigid with anger, and it occurs to me that he may well be lying to Jack and there is no apology coming. No doubt when tomorrow comes he will have come up with something else.

Yeah, my legal team is working on a package, yeah, it's going to be huge, but they can't talk about it until all the legal details are resolved.

Clearly, to Mike, lying is as easy as breathing is to the rest of us. I need to get my phone and check at my end. Fiona would have texted or called. I've only taken one step when Madison's voice booms at the top of the stairs.

"What do you think you're doing?"

She's looking right at me and my stomach does a back flip because I've been caught. I can feel my cheeks blushing crimson. I can tell from the tingle spreading over my face.

"I'm waiting for your dad to finish, that's all." I don't look in her direction, I am too busy to indulge in such juvenile games.

"No you're not, you're listening at the door!" she shrieks. I want to say something back, something clever, something justifying, something that will shut her up, like *Oh, go read your wall, Madison,* but the words don't come and Mike's office door opens. With the phone still cradled in the bend of his neck, he frowns at me and motions me inside with the crook of a forefinger. I don't look back at Madison as I go in and close the door behind me. I pretend it was the plan all along.

"Okay, Jack, I will. You too, buddy." After he hangs up, he sits down heavily and rubs his hands on the top of his thighs. "It's going to be okay. God! What a relief!"

Am I hearing him right? Is that it? I go through all this, I dig up bodies in the dead of night, I talk to the press, then Mike just waves a magic wand and everything is okay again?

"It is?" I ask. I try to inject some enthusiasm in my tone, even though I can feel the corners of my mouth pull down, like I'm about to cry.

"Alex Pace has secured a retraction and apology. They're printing it tomorrow," he says.

"Really? Wow, that's great, Mike, I'm really happy for you."

"Are you?"

I cock my head at him. Something in his eyes creeps me out. I cross my arms. Defiant. "Of course! You know I am. Why would you ask?"

But a small sliver of doubt has creeped in my mind. *Has Fiona said anything? That it was me?* I return the small smile but mine is tight and forced.

"Because I've been racking my brain, trying to figure out who knew so much, all that detail coming together like that, in the article." His eyes are fixed on mine, in a kind of unspoken blinking competition.

I blink first because you have to pick your battles and he's welcome to that one.

"And? What have you come up with?" There's a small twitch on my upper lip. Something that only happens when I'm nervous. I rub two fingers along the corners of my mouth.

He lifts his hands, palms up, shakes his head. "Search me."

"Well, I'm glad it's over."

"Me too." He claps his hands together and swivels in his chair so his back is to me. "Not quite over. Alex is negotiating a payout as we speak."

"Oh, really?"

"You bet. And it'll be significant. They've trashed my reputation and that doesn't come cheap. It's going to cost me some hard-earned money in lost business, and I'm going to get back, trust me on that."

I'm screwed. I knew I should never have recorded that

stupid video. Oh my God. I don't know what to do. Mike will take them to court, and they'll use my video statement as their defense. Everyone will know, that it was me. Maybe I should talk to Alex Pace. Explain. Ask him to do something so it doesn't go this far.

Mike swivels his chair back to me, surprised that I'm still here. "Everything okay?" he asks.

No. Everything is not okay. Everything is fucked, actually.

"Yes, fine, sorry, deep in thought. I'll leave you to it," I say, brightly.

I fully expect to find Madison outside the door, but she's gone. I wonder what Ms. Victoria Secret will make of Madison? That brings a small smile to my lips.

Later, I call Fiona.

"Did you tell him it was me?" I blurt out when she picks up.

"What?"

"Did you tell my husband that it was me, who spoke to you?"

"What do you take me for? Of course not. I haven't spoken to your husband. We have lawyers for that."

"Did they know? That it was me?"

"Hey, Tamra, if you can stop thinking about yourself for a second—"

"Does anyone know it was me!" I shout.

"No! No one knows but me, okay? That's how it works. But I'm in big trouble with my boss, in case you're interested. Your lawyers—"

"They're not my lawyers."

"Your *husband's* lawyers have pulled out the heavy artillery. Only a full retraction and a sincere and detailed apology will do. You're sure this really happened, Tamra? Because normally, we might get asked to issue a correction, but your husband seems real confident of his position."

"Did you go to the clinic?"

"Yes! What do you think? Nothing, zilch, nada. Management denies she was ever there."

"I told you, that's because—"

"Yeah, because the doctor in charge performed the operation and did not keep records in exchange for a fee. But you don't even have a name for that doctor, Tamra. I've spoken to all the doctors I could, and no one will admit to performing abortions in secret for an extra fee, or off the record, if that's the term."

"He's not going to admit it to a journalist, is he?"

"Every one of the doctors there asked the same thing: Why would a health professional put themselves in that position? Abortion isn't illegal, there's no reason to perform it in secret in a back alley somewhere. What if something went wrong? What if the patient went home and bled to death?"

I grit my teeth in frustration. "Because Mike didn't want to risk it," I hiss into the phone. "I explained all that already. He paid handsomely so that her visit was never recorded."

I can hear her sigh at the end of the line.

"There's no CCTV, Tamra."

"Sure there is! I saw the cameras!"

"Not after two years. They don't keep data that long."

Shit. This is really bad news.

"Do you have anything else? I need a name for that doctor, someone. Anyone that will corroborate what you told me."

"Did you check the clinic's bank records?"

"I may have had a guy look into it, yes, and he may

have come back to me saying there's nothing to see there, nothing out of the ordinary. No red flags."

This is so wrong. There's got to be something. "You've got to keep looking, okay? I'm telling you the truth!"

"So bring me something, Tamra. I'm not going to lose my job over this just to protect you."

I can't begin to imagine what Mike is going to do to me if he finds out I'm behind the article. And he gets away with it? This was not supposed to happen this way.

Afterward, I have this strange feeling with me all day— something Fiona said that tickles the edge of my consciousness, but I can't put my finger on it.

Chapter Fourteen

I'm on the phone with Lauren; she talks about lawyers, settlements. How dare they? She's so outraged it almost makes me feel guilty. "I know Mike is no saint," she says, "but this is something else. I'm so angry I could scream. I've called and left a message for that bitch Fiona Martin–"

"You did what?" I blurt, my voice an octave higher than normal.

"I told her, you can't print gossips and lies like that, there are consequences. This is unacceptable–"

"No Lauren, please, I know you mean well but don't call the papers, you'll make it worse! Mike's onto it, really, his lawyer's already–"

The doorbell rings, interrupting our conversation, and I just know it's them. Even before I hear the loud bangs on the door. I tell Lauren that I'll call her back and hang up.

Madison materializes at the top of the stairs and I stare at her, and she stares at me, and there's a split second where it feels like we know exactly what the other one is thinking. It's the best communication we've ever had.

Before I have time to reach the front door, Mike's office

door has flung open. He sees me, and we both freeze. Madison's flown down the stairs and she's the one who greets the cops.

"We have a lot more questions, Mr. Mitchell," O'Brien says. It's nothing like last time. There's no pat on the back, *you're just doing your job, detective*, this time it's silent warfare on both sides.

Mike asks if he can have a lawyer present and they say yes, if you must, and I volunteer to call Alex Pace.

"He's not a criminal lawyer," Mike whispers to me.

"He'll know one. I'll take care of it," I whisper back.

At first, he hesitates, but then he relents, nods. Mike insist that Madison go back upstairs to her room, but she wants to sit in, and he tells her it's out of the question. Her little chin trembles and she looks twelve, but she does what she's told.

Mike takes the cops to the front room and closes the door, and I grab the handset from the living room, the one that sits in a cradle and that we rarely use since we all have cell phones. I dial the number and just as the call is picked up, I press the mute button, ready for one of my finest performances. That's how good I am. I actually prepare for the extremely unlikely eventuality that Mike will later check that I made the call, and how long I was on the phone.

I ask for Alex Pace, I tell my imaginary friend in a voice that cracks with anxiety that it's really urgent, and yes, I understand that he's not there, and he's not reachable right now, but if she could give him the message as a matter of urgency, I'd really appreciate it. She's hung up by then. She could only say 'hello? Can you hear me? Are you there?' so many times.

Then I check my fingernails for any dirt, just to pass

the time, really, because I know they're really clean, I mean I'm not some trailer trash, not anymore anyway. I wonder if I'll get half of everything in the divorce now? When he's found guilty and goes to jail for murder? Or will it be more? I ponder what kind of house I might buy, until I decide I've played long enough and I knock on the door of the small sitting room.

Mike's face is white. His lips are a thin line, and while his chin juts forward, I see he's making a show of being super relaxed and completely in control. I can tell how scared he is—it's all I can do to stop myself from grinning.

"He'll be here as soon as he can," I say, somber.

"Mr. Mitchell, I'll be straight with you. We couldn't care less what you get up to in your personal life as long as it's not illegal. No offense, Ma'am," he says to me, as an afterthought.

"None taken," I say sweetly. Because hey, no big deal, right? I can feel rather than see Mike next to me release his breath, like a punctured balloon.

"Mrs. Mitchell," O'Brien calls out as I recede from the room. "Can we ask you a couple of questions?"

Mike objects, but I give him a very small nod as if to say, *don't worry babe, I know to keep my mouth shut.*

"Yes, of course. Happy to help. What's this about?" I ask.

"It's about Ms. Charlene Donovan. Remember her?" she says. Does she mean to make a joke?

"Yes, of course, but that's all sorted. You should have called and saved yourselves the trouble. The paper is printing a retraction and an apology, isn't that right, darling?" I say, feeling inspired.

"Yes, that's right," he says in a surprisingly confident voice.

"A retraction?" Torres directs the question to Mike.

"That's right. Now if that'll be all—"

"Did you have an affair with Charlene Donovan and then provide an abortion for her? Mr. Mitchell?" Torres asks.

Suddenly we've all forgotten that we're waiting for a lawyer that's not coming, because Mike has sprung from his chair.

"Absolutely, categorically not." And I have to say, I'm a little impressed, a little turned on even, by how easily he can lie. I think you could strap a lie detector on him right here and right now, and he'd pass.

"And I thought you weren't interested in my private life," he sneers. A mistake I think. He can't have it both ways, either he did have an affair, or he didn't. But he keeps going through a diatribe of denials, complete with barely hidden legal threats.

"That has nothing to do with me, you hear?" He makes wide gestures with his arms, hands flat, like he's cutting grass or something. "Nothing! And you have no right to suggest otherwise!"

"We're not suggesting you had anything to do with it, Mr. Mitchell," Torres says, his arms resting on his knees, which I notice is a favorite position for him. "Sit down, Mr. Mitchell," he adds. "We just want to ask a couple of questions, then we'll be out of your hair, is that all right with you?"

Mike sits back down, and he nods quickly. "All right," he says.

Then we go around in circles. They keep asking the same questions and he gives variations on the same answers. It goes on and on. Did Mike ever have sexual relations with Charlene Donovan? (No). Did he know she came back to North Carolina? (No). Had she been in touch with him at all after she returned to Texas? (Absolutely not).

Then Torres turns to me. "Were you aware of the rumors about your husband and Ms. Donovan?"

Mike interjects with a stern "Please don't harass my wife, Officer Torres, or we'll have to stop right now."

He nods and exchanges a look with O'Brien.

"You used to own a house near the Uwharrie Forest, didn't you?" she asks.

Mike says he doesn't think he should have to answer that question, but I've already blurted out, "Yes."

"Why did you sell it?" That question is directed at me.

"My husband owned the house before we were married," I say. "The kids loved spending time there, but they're all grown up now—" and I resist the urge to look up in the direction of Madison's bedroom, "—and really, the house was too big for just the two of us, by that stage." Mike nods a lot at that and doesn't notice O'Brien gazing around her, taking in the size and opulence of our home. I know what she's thinking. *That other house must have been like a fucking castle if they think it was too big.*

"Whose decision was it?" O'Brien asks.

"To sell the house? Mike's," I say, just as Mike says, "Tamra's."

I feel myself go bright red. "I guess it was a mutual decision," I say, but it's too late. Mike's face is rigid with anger. His eyes have grown dark and I desperately try to back-pedal. I tell them that it'd been an ongoing discussion, and it was two years ago so it's hard to remember.

"Detective, my wife is being coy here. The fact is that Deborah, my ex-wife and the mother of my children, and I bought that house, and Deb decorated it. Tamra hated it because of that. She always complained that it reminded her of my past. I didn't want to sell it, I loved that house in fact, but in the end, it wasn't worth the grief."

A wave of crimson rises up my throat and I'm speechless by the audacity of his words. They're all staring at me. I should say something, I want to stand up and shout in Mike's face that he is the world's biggest asshole, but in the end, I just give quick shakes of the head, stare into my lap, and knot my hands together, trying to keep the well of hot tears from rising.

"We need to know where you've been, from last Monday morning until Wednesday morning. Both of you. Can you write down the times, who you were with, and where you were? We'll pick it up this afternoon."

"Why?" Mike asks, his tone dripping with outrage while I bite my bottom lip.

"The victim's body didn't surface of its own accord. Someone dug it up to make sure it was found. Probably Tuesday night, but it could have been earlier. So we want to cover both Monday, and Tuesday."

"Well, that's easy then," Mike declares, crossing one leg over the other. "The three of us were here Monday night."

"Can anyone vouch for that? Outside of you two I mean."

We both look at each other.

"I've had phone conversations with people, I can write that down for you."

Torres makes a note. "Anything else?"

"I was online, on various social accounts, that should help, right?" I say.

Torres nods. "You said that was Monday night? So what about Tuesday night?"

Mike jumps in with "My daughter and I went to a

restaurant. There are plenty of other people there who can vouch for that."

"I thought you said the body was moved Monday night," I say.

"No, I didn't. And I never said it was moved. I said it was unearthed. Did you go to the restaurant as well, Mrs. Mitchell?"

"No. It was a father-daughter evening."

"So you were here by yourself? Can anyone vouch for that?"

"Yes, my friend Lauren. She came by to visit."

Chapter Fifteen

They leave with a 'we'll be in touch later today, don't leave town, thanks for your time.' I let them out and I lean out the door and whisper to O'Brien.

"Are you going to arrest him?"

"Not today."

"Tomorrow? Soon?"

She does a little flick of the head and narrows her eyes at me. "You sound like you want us to, Mrs. Mitchell."

I hiss at her. "No, no, no! Nothing like that. I just want to know, that's all."

"Do you know something?" she asks.

Madison materializes behind me, trying to look like she hasn't been eavesdropping all this time.

"Thank you, Detectives, I hope that puts an end to the matter," I say forcefully before closing the door in her stunned face.

"Dad?" Madison whines.

"Not now, Maddie!" Mike booms, and his tone is so forceful that she retreats immediately, bottom lip quivering.

Mike reaches for the bottle of Scotch that sits atop the

corner bar. I snatch it away from him. "It's only two o'clock in the afternoon! What are you doing?"

His face is ashen. "I—I don't know." He grabs his hair with both hands.

What did you think would happen? I want to tell him. *Did you really think all this would never catch up with you? You can actually sleep at night?*

I rest my hand on his shoulder, my face a picture of innocence. "Don't jump down my throat, but did you do something you shouldn't have?"

His head snaps toward me. "What the fuck does that mean, Tamra?"

"It's a heck of a coincidence, wouldn't you say? That your... that she turns up dead less than two miles from our own house. Isn't it time we talked about this?"

His face distorts. I've never seen him like this before. "No! No, no, no—"

I soften my voice. "Because I'm on your side, no matter what. We're in this together, okay? So you can tell me anything."

He swears to me over and over that he had nothing to do with it. Did you know she was back? I ask. Did she get in touch with you? He swears he's had no contact with her since before the... intervention. That's what he calls the abortion, the intervention.

He pleads with me. He begs me. I have to believe him. If I thought that he was capable of hurting anyone, then he is lost, he says. He has never laid a hand on her, he swears on his children's head, which almost makes me laugh out-loud considering we all know he had sex with her, and probably more than once, but I know he means to say he didn't harm her.

"Tamra, baby doll, you can't think that I'm capable of killing someone!" he whines.

"Maybe we're all capable of murder, given the right circumstances," I reply, trying to stop my eyes from flicking up in the general direction of Madison's bedroom. "You have to come clean, Mike."

"But I keep telling you that I—"

"No, I mean about the—intervention." I have to admit, it does sound better.

"Are you completely crazy? If I admit to that, they'll think I killed her!"

"Yeah, and if you keep denying it and they find out later it was true, how are you going to look then? Think about it! She's dead, Mike! How do you think that looks?"

He turns to me then, his eyes dark. "Why did you say that, in there? That it was my idea to sell the house?"

I give a small shrug, look away. "I got flustered," I say.

"Flustered? How can you get flustered about something like that? We agreed, Tamra! I didn't want to sell the house, you know it was you!"

I'm speechless. I stare at him, my jaw slack with shock. His narrowed eyes are daring me to contradict him. All of a sudden I feel nauseous.

"Don't look at me like that," he says. "I went along with it because you convinced me. I didn't want to sell it, in fact I would have much preferred to keep that house."

I just can't believe what I'm hearing. For a moment I think I'm going crazy. Could he really have forgotten what happened that summer?

Slowly, deliberately, I explain to him in words that I think he should be able to understand. "We sold the house to get her money together, Mike, remember?"

He motions to me to keep my voice down.

"We had to sell it, you know that." I say the words again slowly, deliberately, and softly.

"You never cared for that house," he snaps. Which is true. That house was part of his history, his First Family, and I couldn't stand being there, but it's also completely beside the point.

"We needed the money fast, remember?"

"That may be true, but we could have gotten it another way."

"We went over that, Mike. It was the easiest and quickest way to get our hands on it." *And it was all your fault*, I want to add.

"So why did you say that it was me just now?" he asks. "We'd agreed, if it ever came up, if anyone asked, we sold it because the kids had moved on."

"And that's what I said."

"No, that's not what you said! You put it all on me! That I wanted to sell it! That it was my idea!"

"And you made it sound like I couldn't live with your past! All that crap about Deborah and that I couldn't bear it!"

"Well, that's the truth, isn't it?"

"You didn't have to tell them!"

"And if you had stuck to the story in the first place, I wouldn't have! Christ! It's like I'm talking to a brick wall!"

It was probably a mistake, I realize that now, but it's too late. I can't change it. "Look, I'm sorry! I'll tell them it was me, okay?"

"Yeah, and how's that going to look?" He smirks.

I turn to face him more fully. He's shaking. He's lost, I suddenly realize. And very frightened.

"I haven't done anything, Tamra. I swear it. Please believe me."

Wow. I am staring in the eyes of the devil himself.

"So how do you explain it?" I ask.

"I don't know, don't you see? Maybe my competitors are trying to frame me?"

True to form, Mike takes it back to Mike. Not a thought for the poor girl, or her mom and dad who have just learned that their missing daughter is never coming home.

"What about you?" he asks.

"What about me?"

"Did you ever talk to her? After that night?"

I can't help it, my eyes widen, and I blink a few times. He's still looking up at me, expectantly. Waiting for an answer.

"Did you know she came back?" he asks. "If you do, tell me!"

My God. I shake my head in disbelief. This man is something else. I'm starting to suspect I'm dealing with a psychopath. He knows very well that wouldn't be possible, that she never came back, because she never went away in the first place.

"No."

He leans back in his chair and looks at the ceiling.

Then it comes to me. "You need to get in touch with her parents."

"Are you out of your mind?" he growls.

"Offer your condolences. That's the first thing. The article's out there now. You need to get on the front foot on this one, Mike."

He rubs a hand across his eyes, then he says, "I don't understand what's happening, Tamra," in a voice thick with fear that I don't recognize, and it makes my heart break. Because after everything I've done for him, the ways I have stood by him, in ways he doesn't even know about, and for all the hurt he has lashed down upon me, I still love him.

Just kidding.

Chapter Sixteen

It was almost the end of summer, the year before last. Mike had been talking with Pastor Frank about the possibility of running for governor, but he wasn't telling anyone yet. But something changed in him. He became moody. He'd be lost in his own world and I'd have to repeat myself whenever I wanted his attention.

I'll never forget the shock of finding out. We were out for dinner, something we did often, but it hadn't been as enjoyable as usual. We were waiting for the check, and he excused himself to use the men's room. His cell phone was on the table, and when it chimed with a text, I picked it up.

> Don't delay for too long handsome, the window is not going to stay open forever xox C.

When he got back to the table, I'd already left. That night we had the biggest fight we've ever had. I kept waiting for him to explain, tell me something that would make sense, convince me that this wasn't the biggest betrayal of my life, but instead he just sat there, with his head in hands. Then he looked up and said, "There's something I have to tell you."

So he told me. It happened once, and once only, he swore to me. He said that she had seduced him. That she was a monster in sheep's clothing and that's probably the only part of that sorry tale I believed. When he said that she was pregnant, my heart just broke into a million little pieces. In that moment, I thought he was telling me he was leaving me to start a new life with that girl and their baby. The baby that he'd said he and I couldn't have because, *I love you so much, I don't want to share you with anyone else.*

But no, he really wanted my help. He had been tricked, he said. They'd been at a dinner, a working dinner he said, whatever the fuck that means. I mean, what kind of work do these people actually do at dinner where they drink so much that they end up in bed together five minutes after dessert?

He was lost. He had gone to Pastor Frank to confess, that's what he said—although as it turned out, it was more of a "help-me-father-for-she-has-sinned" kind of confession. Pastor Frank told Mike that the devil presented himself in many guises, and that a young woman inspiring lustful thoughts was one of his usual tricks. The way Mike told it, Pastor Frank had assured him he was being way too hard on himself, and he shouldn't shoulder all the blame, considering.

Considering what? I asked.

"You haven't seen her, so you don't understand," he replied. She was out to get him from the first day. She must have targeted him. For money, blackmail, power, the usual. And there are always people only too happy to stab you in the back in this business, and she could well have been planted by one of them.

I nodded. Did it make sense? Not really, but it made me feel better to think that he had been set up. I was still crushed, I was still numb from shock, but by then he was on his knees, with both hands gripping mine, and he swore to me that he had never done anything like this before, and it had only happened that one time, and that he would do anything to make it up to me.

But what about the pregnancy? I asked.

She's having an abortion, he replied.

Oh my God! Really?

It's going to cost us half a million dollars, but yes.

Us?

So she really was after the money, I murmured.

I told you, she's a scam artist, he said.

And I knew he was right. Someone who agrees to be paid all that money to have an abortion is not a victim. As scams go, if you have no morals whatsoever, it's not a bad one. You could move onto the next target in a matter of weeks.

Was he absolutely sure she was telling the truth? I had to ask. The odds of getting pregnant after just one sexual encounter are pretty slim.

He was sure.

So that's it? You give her half a million dollars and she will go away?

That's exactly it, he'd said.

And suddenly I was lightheaded with relief. She was an awful person, depraved even. She'd lured him into a trap and he was powerless because he was weak. It takes a certain type of man to withstand the siren song of a beautiful, young enchantress, and Mike was not that type of man. I knew that, and so be it. But he had been tricked, and he had learned his lesson.

We may live comfortably, but half a million bucks is not pocket change, that's for sure, and we didn't have that much money in cash lying around, and after a couple of hours of recriminations, tears, and begging for forgiveness, we came to the conclusion that we had to sell the Badin Lake house as quickly as possible.

He kissed me, full on the mouth, and he tasted like rain. We made love, right there on the rug, and he held me tight and whispered words that were so sweet I was delirious with happiness. It reminded me of when we first met, that obsessive love, and for a while, I actually thought that betrayal was a godsend. We had come through the biggest crisis of our marriage, stronger than ever. We were a team, Mike and I, and we were going to get through this together. I remember thinking that night, as I lay in his arms, my head on his bare chest, that you can't fake that kind of love.

Then he said, there's one small thing, and I need you, my darling. I need you so much, and you're the only one who can help me.

What is it? I asked.

Chapter Seventeen

Was it really *just once?* As if. More like the duration of her employment. And I bet she hadn't been the first, either. Nor the last, as I now know, in spite of his tearful, pseudo-heartfelt promises.

We booked her in for the abortion; it was the end of the internship by that stage. We sold the Badin Lake house and Mike bought her a plane ticket back to Austin.

When he sobs in my arms in the middle of the night, and he says that he doesn't understand what's happening, I can't help wondering whether he was under some kind of spell that night. What he did to her was so sickening that he has wiped it from his mind. Because it's like he literally does not remember.

I am going to church. Not to pray, because I don't need to go to church for that, but to see Pastor Frank. I need his help. I tell Mike I want to get his advice and he thinks that is a great idea. He would go himself, but he doesn't want to get out of the house right now. He doesn't want anyone to take his picture and plaster it all over the internet. Not until we've planned exactly what we're going to say.

But it's not Pastor Frank's advice that I'm after, it's his help. Because I'm sick and tired of Mike digging his heels in, and I don't have time for this. He had the affair; she had the abortion, and it never occurred to me he would straight up deny it when confronted by the cops. Or the press. If I can't prove it to Fiona Martin, it's all been for nothing, and there's no way I'm going to let that happen. This is not a freaking tale of redemption, it's a *revenge* story.

So now I'm here, because let's face it, Pastor Frank is up to his neck in this almost as much as Mike is.

Apparently, it was Pastor Frank's idea that Mike run for governor. I'm not completely sure why; I think it has to do with state tax laws or something equally selfish and non-Christian. Mike thought it was a stroke of genius, or maybe an order from God, and he put everything in motion. They wouldn't announce it until the campaign, which at that stage wasn't for another eighteen months at least. But then Charlene told him the happy news: that she was going to have his baby. And that, was not part of the strategy.

So when Mike confessed his sins to Pastor Frank, Pastor Frank told him that it took two to tango, and it happened all the time, and as long as no one found out, there was no reason for him to change his plans. Mike told him about Charlene's offer—half a mil, and the little problem would go away. Pastor Frank said he knew just the place. A clinic that could take care of everything, and they were very, very discreet. In fact, so discreet that no official records would be kept at all.

Maybe I should have been shocked that Pastor Frank could be advocating such a thing, but it was quite the opposite. It made me feel like we had been validated. If Pastor Frank was going to help us put this sorry business out of our way, then she must be the devil incarnate, and he should know. That was his business, after all.

"You've seen the article, I take it," I say to Pastor Frank now. We're sitting in his office, I in the armchair and he behind the desk, his fingers together in a steeple.

He nods. "It's a terrible business, all this. Just terrible. Do you have any idea who leaked it?"

Leaked it. What an odd thing to say.

"Not yet. But the police came to see us."

He jumps. "Did my name come up?"

"No. Of course not. Why would it?" Actually, come to think of it, there are very good reasons why it would.

"Good, good. I can't be associated with this sordid business, you understand? Who spoke to the reporter in the first place, do you know?"

"No."

He says nothing for a moment, but he looks worried. He should be, but he has not mentioned that she was dead yet, not once.

"Pastor Frank…"

"I think you can drop the Pastor for now."

I nod. "Mike doesn't want to admit to the abortion."

He scoffs. "I hope not! He's absolutely right! He mustn't admit to anything! Can you imagine what would happen if people found out? It would end his career!"

And yours, too, Pastor, don't forget that, I think, although I don't say it out loud.

"But it's out in the open now. Someone with information has told that reporter. The police are going to want to talk to that person, and at some point, it's going to come out that it was true, don't you see? This is what I'm worried about! How is it going to look if that happens, and Mike has been trying to bury it? It's better if he talks to the police. And I'll be by his side. If we're upfront. Then we can control the story. Right now, it's completely out of our hands. Mike won't listen to me. You have to talk to him and convince him."

"No. Absolutely not. I'm with Mike on this one, Tamra. There's nothing to be gained by bringing up the whole sordid mess."

"Except it's been brought up already."

"And it will go away. I've seen it happen many times, you'll see. Just sit tight, that's what you have to do, the both of you. You're not thinking of taking matters in your own hands, are you?"

I cock my head at him. There's a bit of perspiration on his top lip. I wonder if I'm making him nervous. "She's been murdered, Frank. You honestly believe that it will go away?"

That makes him wince, and I honestly can't tell if it's because I brought up her murder, or because I used the Lord's son's name in vain. "I really think Mike should own up."

He stands up, walks around the desk and sits beside me, in the other armchair. "All of us are sinners," he says, his tone soothing. Reasonable. "Our faith, our evangelical faith is based on forgiveness. As you well know. It's not our place to judge. Not yours, not mine."

"But the girl is dead! Why is it you can't see that? Either of you! It changes everything, don't you see?"

"It would ruin Mike's chances, completely and categorically. He would be out of the race before it even started."

"In the scheme of things, does it really matter?"

"He's the best we've got. We need men like Mike—strong, principled men," he says, and with a straight face, too. "We can't let this incident ruin his career. Let it be, Tamra. There's nothing to be gained from stirring up trouble. God can forgive small transgressions."

"Small transgression? Is that what you call it?"

He sighs, reaches for my hand and pats it. "It takes two to tango, you know. Don't forget that."

I pull it away. "So I heard. She was twenty years old. Can you imagine how her parents must feel?"

"But her untimely death has nothing to do with us. The police will find out who committed this terrible crime, but it has nothing to do with Mike!" Then it's like a shadow passes over his face, and he says, "Doesn't it?"

I raise my eyebrows and my eyes are big and round. I mean to convey something like, *Oh Lord, could Mike be mixed up in this?* But he misunderstands me because he pats my hand again and says, "I see I've shocked you and I apologize, I shouldn't have asked that. But you see? It would do no good to muddy the waters."

Then he stands, and I know that I've lost that battle.

"Don't worry, please, Tamra. Everything will be fine. Just pray that they catch the man who did this."

Don't pray too hard, I almost say.

Chapter Eighteen

I don't go back home right away. I can't stand it anymore, being cooped up with those two and their miserable faces. But I need to see Lauren. I really need a friend. Plus, I need to ask her something.

"Oh, my God. Are you okay? Come in!" She throws her arms around me, breathless, big and loud, and engulfs me. I can barely breathe, and I love it.

"You don't mind I just showed up on your doorstep like that?" I finally ask once she releases me from her iron hug.

"You're kidding? Come here!"

We sit outside, in her lovely garden; she brings me a tall glass of ice tea.

"Dwayne is still away?"

"Yep," she says. Something passes over her eyes, she looks sad.

"Everything okay?" I ask, just as she asks, "How are you holding up?"

We burst into laughter, in the way only close friends do, and it takes a while to breathe, but it's so nice to laugh.

I never told Lauren what happened with Charlene. I

thought about it, but I didn't say anything because I was embarrassed. I had worked so hard to become the wife I thought Mike wanted.

When Mike met me, I wore miniskirts and chewed gum. I'll never forget our engagement party. It happened in the ballroom of an elegant hotel. I was twenty-six years old and probably old enough to know better. I wore a one-shoulder gold sequin top and a black leather miniskirt, black stockings with the seam at the back, and a pair of Giuseppe Zanotti gold sandals with five-inch stilettos. I thought I looked like a million bucks. Then, when I saw how everyone else was dressed—his friends' wives in their designer evening clothes, stylish and elegant—I felt the wave of shame engulf me.

I ran into the ladies' room. When I caught sight of myself in the mirror, I looked like a sad clown, with my mascara smudged under my eyes and my bright red lipstick smeared across my mouth. I pulled off my Cartier Trinity Ruban engagement ring, threw it in the toilet, and locked myself in a stall.

I heard someone come in, and there was a knock at the door in front of me.

"Go away!" I sobbed.

"Hey girlfriend, you're gonna woman up? Or what?" a voice said.

She spoke like me. I was so shocked, I had to see what she looked like. I opened the door, and there was Lauren, in the most gorgeous evening gown, waving a joint right in front of the *no-smoking* sign. She handed it to me, and I took it, gratefully. In her other hand she had a bottle of Moet & Chandon and two flutes. We squeezed ourselves into the stall, and I sat on the toilet seat while she leaned against the door.

"I feel like a piece of trash," I wailed between champagne refills. "You can take the girl out of the trailer, but you can't take the trash out of the girl," I added. "I bet that's what everyone is saying about me, right this minute."

"No, they're not," she said, the joint between her lips. "They're not bad people. And anyway, look at you! You look fantastic."

I don't know how she did it, but she convinced me that I looked wonderful, that I looked alive, unlike some women out there who looked like cadavers, she said. No wonder Mike fell head over heels for me. Everyone could see how enraptured he was with me. We were very lucky to have each other.

"What did you do with your ring?" she asked, looking at my hands, eyebrows knotted together.

"I'm sitting on it," I said.

Fortunately, I hadn't flushed. She made me reach in and get it. We laughed so much I almost peed myself. Then she brought me in front of the mirror, fixed my makeup, and told me to woman up.

Needless to say, we've been friends ever since.

Now it feels like that was a million years ago, as I tell her everything that's happened. I tell her that Mike thinks he will get a retraction, but the cops are beginning to suspect him. I watch the shock mount over her face until it's me who embraces her.

"Oh, girlfriend, that must be horrible, having the cops in your house like that, asking all these vile questions. Is there anything I can do?" She moves a strand of hair away from my face.

"Actually, there is."

"Shoot," she says, inappropriately.

"You remember the other night, I told you Mike and

Madison went out and I stayed home? Well, the problem is, it would make my life easier if you could verify that. It's the only night I can't prove where I was and the cops won't stop bugging me otherwise."

"You're kidding! Why?"

I explain to her about the body having been dug up. "They don't think it's me!" I laugh, more like a bark really, "It's just that I was on my own. Oh, Christ, I can't believe I just said those words." I bite my bottom lip. "Can you say that you came by, if they ask?"

She flicks a hand in the air. "Is that it? Yes, of course."

I let out a breath that makes my body deflate in relief. I hadn't realized how stressed I'd been about that.

"Is it true?" she asks in a voice almost conspiratorial.

I flinch. "Of course! How can you ask me that? Where do you think I was—"

"No, no, no." She waves her hands in front of her face. "He had an affair with this girl? Is it true?"

I look at my hands. "Yes."

She snorts, and when I look at her, I'm surprised to see tears in her eyes.

"Hey, Lauren, what's wrong?"

She quickly brushes her fingers over her eyes. "Sorry. I'm really emotional at the moment."

"You're okay?"

"I should be asking you that," she says, chuckling.

"I'll be fine." I pat her knee, squeeze her hand.

"And the abortion?"

I hesitate, but only for a second. "Yes."

"Oh, Tamra! How did you find out?"

"It's complicated."

"I'll bet."

"You won't tell anyone what I just said, will you?" I ask.

"It's on the front page of the Tribune, Tamra. Who can I possibly tell?" She lets out a small puff of air. "I can't believe that he had an affair, got her to have an abortion, and then he told you all about it! That's just too much. What a piece of shit."

"What makes you think he told me?"

She scoffs. "How else would you have found out?"

"*She* might have told me."

"Except she's... you know... dead," she says. "You need to move out. You can't stay there. It's getting from bad to worse, girlfriend. You have to come and stay here."

Is that what I should do? I don't think so. Keep your enemies close. That's what they say. I can do more at home to get what I ultimately want than if I move out.

"Are you listening?" Her face is inches from mine. She's looking intently into my eyes.

I shake my head. "Sorry. What did you say?"

"Where were you the other night? When I came by?"

"I told you. I went to sleep really early."

"For real? Because you know, it's not like you. You can tell me, you know," she adds. Obviously she's not thinking that I went out for a bit of body retrieval. Maybe she thinks I went to a bar, or something.

"There's nothing to tell! So much going on, I was out to the world. That and a couple drinks." I smile, sheepish. "Okay, maybe more than a couple." I take a sip of my iced tea.

She nods.

"So if they ask—"

She puts a hand on my arm and pats it. "Relax. We spent the evening together."

Chapter Nineteen

I bring up Madison. Why? Because I can't get her out of my head.

"Mike might think it's great and she looks great and she's a young woman, that's what they do, but it wasn't that long ago that I was a young woman, not unlike Madison. I know an eating disorder when I see one. I did a bit of googling and as it happens," I pull up my phone and show Lauren a webpage, "Look at this. It's a treatment center, for eating disorders. Just a few miles from here, see? It looks good. We'd have to check it out, and she'll need to be assessed I guess, but—"

"You're crazy. Madison is never going to speak to you again if you show her that." She points to the phone. The page that shows a healthy young woman, all smiles and ruddy cheeks.

I sigh. "Will you talk to her?" I ask, reluctantly.

"Of course. I'd be happy to," she replies, and I don't know why but I feel a touch of annoyance. I think because she so readily accepts that she's better placed than me to do so. And then she adds, "But I'm not convinced she needs it." And I want to ask, *so what do you suggest? Because that girl is not well, and everyone putting their head in the sand isn't going to change that.*

In the end, I decide to go and check out the treatment center on the way home, and mull over the likelihood of success all the way there. Because Lauren's probably right. I can't imagine it's going to do any good, but I'm hoping the *Rule of 7* really does work. I read it on a marketing advice blog, although why I was reading a marketing advice blog is anyone's guess. Anyway, from memory, by the time you've heard of some useless thing seven times, you want one. That's the critical mass, the seventh time.

Back home, armed with my pile of helpful pamphlets, I pop into the Room of Wise Sayings and pull open various drawers to find a book, or a magazine, anything that she might pick up to read, and where I can slip my pamphlets and hope she'll find them. It will be only the first of seven, but you have to start somewhere. On her dresser I spot my Pandora bracelet. I know it's mine because I recognize the charms. I haven't worn it in years. I grab it and shove it in my pocket.

I'm rifling through a pile of what looks like old mail in a drawer of her desk. Something catches my eye. It's a notice from her university, and the way it's folded, the date and the first paragraph is clearly visible. It's dated two months ago.

Dear Ms. Mitchell,

We acknowledge receipt of your letter informing us of your withdrawal from the Masters of Business Administration program. Please note no fees will be refunded and you will be charged a $75 withdrawal fee. However you may be eligible for a partial tuition refund as per the University Credit Balances and Refunds Policy.

We wish you well in your future endeavors.

My jaw drops. I sit on the side of her bed holding the letter in my hand. I have to read it three times to make sure I understand correctly. Madison has withdrawn from her college degree, and she has not told anyone. So what is she doing now?

I asked her the other day, how long she was staying with us. I thought she should have gone back already—it's not a long break, but she shrugged me off and said she did so well on her exams she could go back late. And she wanted to stay here, look after her dad. He needed her.

I had no reason to doubt her. There's a part of me that insists this is none of my business, but the other part is screaming at me that something is very wrong here. Only a few days ago, Madison was cuddled up with her father on the couch singing the praises of her courses, discussing the minutiae of the curriculum. So, what's going on?

I hurry back downstairs, and I make the call before I have the time to change my mind. The phone number is in Mike's office, on a Post-it note that has curled with time but is still stuck on the rim of the bookshelf.

"Hello?"

"Is this Deborah?" I have never called the first Mrs. Mitchell. I've never had the occasion. And for a bizarre moment I'm pleased to hear her voice, because we are going to talk about Madison. Maybe I could call her Maddie. We're going to talk about what we're going to do to help this kid. She may not be a kid anymore, but she sure acts like one.

"Who is this?"

"It's Tamra." Should I add, *Mitchell*?

"Who?"

Yes, I should.

"Tamra Mitchell." I hear her intake of breath, like a small shock absorber.

"I'm calling about Madison." I have no intention of mentioning the university withdrawal, the lies, etcetera. I'm more concerned about her anorexia. I've left the pamphlet among that pile of mail, and her mother and I can team up to take care of the rest.

"What's happened?"

"Oh no, nothing, well not exactly, it's just that I'm really worried about her, Deborah. About her weight problem."

"Excuse me?"

Well, I have to say, I expected something different from her. I don't know what exactly, but definitely different. "You know that Madison is suffering from an eating disorder, don't you? When's the last time you saw her?"

"Are you completely crazy? How dare you call me and speak to me like that! You're a home-wrecker, Tamra. If it were up to me, my daughter wouldn't spend a single second in that house with you. I only let her because she insists on that relationship with her cheating, lying father and I can't stop her. But now you call *my* house? Go jump in a lake, Tamra *Mitchell*."

Mike always told me that the divorce had been amicable. That was his word: Amicable. That they'd grown apart, and by the time I came along, they'd been going through the motions of separation. He spent time at the house for the sake of the children, even though only Madison was still living at home. I didn't question it. Why would I? It wasn't in my favor. I wasn't there to provide reconciliation advice; I was there to take him for myself—

legally, preferably—and if that could happen without rancor, who was I to argue?

But I have to say, things don't look amicable from where I'm standing. I take the Pandora bracelet back to my room and slip it in the bedside table. That's when I spot the Glock. Mike keeps it for protection, even though I don't like it in the house. He left it out on the desk the other day, and I placed it in my drawer. Now I'm thinking, it's too exposed. Too accessible. If Madison rummaged through my stuff and took my Pandora bracelet, wait till she finds this. I shudder. I decide to move it and make a mental note to tell him later. The Glock ends up in a shoe box on the bottom shelf of the closet.

Chapter Twenty

Mike doesn't want to do the press conference. He thinks it's the wrong message. He says he should lie low. It'll blow over, he says.

Yeah, right. Over my dead body.

"I think we've passed that moment," I say. "You need to take control. Be strong, be decisive, now more than ever."

He doesn't look strong and decisive, that's for sure. He looks small, crumpled into a heap. He keeps running a hand through his hair. Every time Madison comes to talk to him, I'm in the doorway in a flash and in my most soothing voice, I whisper, "Not now, Madison."

"Mike, darling, you can't let your fear rule your head. You're the one who taught me that."

He smiles then, maybe not a smile, exactly. More like a lift of the lip. If I didn't know any better, I might have taken it for a sneer. But the look in his eyes becomes softer, almost grateful, and I'm thinking that this is great. I rock at this sort of thing. "I will stand by you, I promise you that. I will do everything in my power to help you, and to guide you, through this difficult time," I continue.

I take his face in both my hands and hold him, gazing into his eyes that by now are swimming. I can't remember the last time I had so much fun.

"Thank you," he says. Then he shakes his head and he adds, "I'm so sorry, Tamra, for everything I've put you through. I don't deserve you." Which makes me think that either The Slut hasn't returned his calls, or he suspects that now that he's officially *a murder suspect*, all bets are off, no matter how much frilly lingerie he throws at her.

God knows I keep looking, keep an eye out. I check his texts whenever I can snatch the phone in time. I check his pockets. If he's still in touch with her, all power to him. She can have him. I just want to make him miserable. And I want his money. She can have whatever's left of him. She can visit him in prison. She and Madison can go together.

We're standing outside our house, Mike and I. It is imperative that I be by his side, although really, I am just one small step behind. But I'm the one who organized the press conference, and I made sure to include Fiona Martin, although I haven't told Mike that.

"You're sure I look okay?" he asks, for the umpteenth time.

"You look fine." I did his makeup. I covered up the dark rings under his eyes and managed to give him a bit of color. The better he looks, the worse it will be, I think.

There are maybe half a dozen journalists, both print and TV. We don't rate that highly in the news cycle. Mike taps the microphone and thanks them for being here.

"First, I want to say how very distressed my family and I were to hear of Ms. Charlene Donovan's violent death. It's a terrible day when a young person's life is snuffed out so soon." He clears his throat, just like he did before, when we rehearsed.

"Earlier today, I spoke to Charlene Donovan's family and offered our sincere condolences for their loss. But this isn't about me," he says, and all the faces that were looking down at their frantic scribblings look up, and I have to bite my tongue to stop myself from bursting out laughing.

"It's about Charlene Donovan, a young woman whose entire future has been robbed from us all, especially from her family. As you know, Charlene Donovan—" He keeps calling her by her full name, as we agreed, because we want to avoid any suggestion of intimacy, even a first name basis. "—worked in my office for the summer, and I remember her as a very bright, ambitious, and capable young woman."

He lifts his eyes from his notes and stands just a little taller.

"Two days ago, a newspaper published a vile and spurious accusation leveled at me. I'm not going to hide or shy away from defending myself, and I intend to do so in a court of law, but I can categorically say, right here and right now, that I have never had a sexual relationship with Ms. Charlene Donovan, and anyone who knows me, knows that I would never do such a thing. The additional accusation that I somehow encouraged Ms. Charlene Donovan to have an abortion is abhorrent to me and to my family. It never happened, and I have instructed my lawyers to pursue charges of libel.

"Let me repeat, this isn't about me; it's about Charlene Donovan." I told him to say that a lot. I said it made him look strong and compassionate. But I think the more he says it, the more it sounds like a lie.

"Her passing affects us all, and it is vitally important

that we catch her killer. If you have any information at all, no matter how small or trivial, please, I implore you, please contact your local police station as soon as you can."

He turns to me, puts out his hand, and calls my name. I smile and step forward, taking his hand in mine in a little flurry of flashes and camera clicks.

"I want to publicly thank my wife, Tamra Mitchell, for her support and her unwavering belief in me." He squeezes my hand and leans in to kiss me on the lips. "I love you. Thank you," he says softly.

Then he stares back toward the cameras, his chin forward, and he points a finger. "If the person who killed this young woman is watching this, then be aware that we will find you. We will track you down, and we will not rest until you have to face justice for this terrible crime."

That was my idea, too. Mike wasn't completely sold on it, but I convinced him that it would make him look strong and determined, and most definitely innocent.

The best part is when Fiona Martin asks, "How do you explain that her body was found near your house?"

I wait for him to answer. After all, we have prepared for that one since it was bound to come up. He's supposed to say that it was not our house when she died. That we had already sold it by then. That it's a minor point, since it's not like she'd been found right there in the front yard; she was at least two miles away from it. But the silence goes on longer than it should, and all eyes are on him now, and he turns on his heel and goes back inside the house, closing the front door after him.

I feel myself blush with embarrassment, left out in the cold like this. I mumble a weak 'sorry' and put my head down. The journalists chat among themselves without so much as a glance in my direction. It seems I am not so newsworthy. Oh wait, that's right, I don't count.

"Are you going to talk to me now?"

I turn around quickly, and it's Fiona Martin, of course. Everyone has meandered away, stepped into their cars or they're walking down the driveway, but there are a couple of stragglers nearby and they glance in our direction. I look her up and down, the way you do when you want to show your contempt.

"I have nothing to say to you."

The stragglers move away and then it's just her and me.

"Why are you protecting him?"

"I'm not."

"You are. That little performance just now." She juts her chin in the direction of the lectern that is still there in front of our porch.

I lean forward a little, even though there's no one around to hear us anymore. "You know why I did that. I have to stand by him. He'll suspect me otherwise."

"Has he said anything?"

"No. He has no idea."

"Be careful, Tamra."

I do a double take, pretend that the realization of what her words imply has just dawned on me. I lean forward, and almost put a hand on her forearm but I stop myself just in time.

"Do you think that I'm in danger?" I let the question trail.

"In your shoes? I would."

I like it. She doesn't know who killed Charlene. I sure haven't told her the rest of my story, yet. But here she is, joining the dots.

I put a hand on my chest, shake my head. She cocks her head and frowns, like she's surprised at how dense I am.

"Have you heard from his lawyers yet?" I ask.

"Interestingly enough, I have not."

"Huh. So he's not feeling quite as confident as he made out. That's good, right?"

Suddenly Lauren's car comes into view, crawling up the driveway.

"I have to go," I tell her, just before jabbing my index finger in the air in front of her face. Then in my strongest, loudest voice, I say, "You come back here and I will call the cops, you hear? You're on my property, lady!"

She gives me a quick, small shake of the head, and just before turning on her heel, she whispers, "Watch your back with him, Tamra, promise me."

With my finger still in her face, I say between clenched teeth, "As long as he doesn't know I'm talking to you, I'll be fine."

Then Lauren's soft-top convertible roars up and almost hits Fiona.

"What's she doing here?" Lauren shoves her thumb toward Fiona's receding back, then she kisses me on one cheek and then the other. "You're okay, girlfriend?"

"Not really," I say, mimicking one of those grimacing face emojis.

The front door opens and Mike stands there, tall and— wait, is that a smile?

I take Lauren's arm into my own. "Don't worry about it. I'm just glad to see you."

I tell her about the press conference, and I make it sound better than it actually was. When we go inside, Mike is gentle. He winks at me, the side of his mouth lifting in the cute way that he does. He's been watching me from the window, I can tell, just as I knew he would. I think it's my finger wagging that did it. I wink back, and he almost laughs.

"Well, people, I brought something to cheer us up. Champagne! And I have sustenance!" Lauren says in a loud voice.

"You know where to go, girlfriend," I say, pushing her playfully. She does a funny walk, with her bags dangling off her fingers that she holds up high.

In a soft voice I say to Mike, "We need all the support we can get, okay? Don't be rude to her. We want as many people on our side as possible."

He nods, then he does something he hasn't done in a very long time. He takes me in his arms, and he pulls me close, resting his chin on top of my head. If I had a knife on me right now, would I slide it into his stomach? I'm not sure.

"I think it went really well, don't you?" I ask.

"It's like a weight has lifted, baby doll. I couldn't have done this without you."

I don't reply. I inhale the scent of him, and I'm hit with a wave of nostalgia, for what we had. For how much he loved me once.

He hugs me tighter. "I love you," he whispers, and we stay like that for a while until he says, "Do you agree that I was right?"

"About which bit?"

"About not telling them what, you know, with the… the intervention."

"No," I say into his neck. "I still think you should."

Madison looks a bit more relaxed than she did before, and I guess that Mike has spoken to her and found the right reassuring words. Lauren has set the table for our lunch: some Venezuelan vegetarian takeout from the new place up the road that personally I think is foul. But now Madison has perked up no end, and she thinks it's *awesome*, and Lauren is a *genius*, and soon they're whispering at the dinner table and as usual I can't help but feel a little hurt.

"I'm really sorry Dwayne couldn't be here," Mike says. "It's been a while since we've seen him. How's he doing?"

She shrugs and even colors a little. She breaks her bread roll into a million pieces. "Hey, you tell me. That man is away on business so often, sometimes I forget what he looks like."

It's funny, but she said the same thing, more or less, the other night at church, and I don't know why this time it sounds contrived. Like it's rehearsed.

"You're okay?" I ask.

"Yeah, why wouldn't I be? It's just a business trip. Don't mind me. I get annoyed with him because he goes away so much, but he promised me it was only two more years."

"He's away for two more years?" Madison asks, eyes wide like saucers.

Lauren slaps her gently on the shoulder, and we laugh because we all know she's joking. Don't we?

"That's what he said. 'Two more years, Lauren, and we won't have to worry about money anymore.'"

"You don't need to worry about money now," I point out.

She shrugs. "Exactly, but you know what these alpha males are like." And she winks at Mike, which makes him laugh. It's such a strange sight, I don't know what to think. Did I miss something? How did they get so buddy-buddy all of a sudden?

Chapter Twenty-One

Mike and I made love last night, and afterward, he held me tightly and whispered words of love in my ear and I couldn't help it. For a few hours I made myself pretend nothing had changed, there was no Slut, and I hadn't dug up poor Charlene. I just wanted to feel happy for a few hours.

It didn't work.

But we agreed that we would go about our business from now on. That we don't need to hide or feel ashamed of ourselves. For Madison, that doesn't mean much since all she does is lounge around the place tethered to her phone, but for Mike, it means putting on his nicest suit and going to the office with his head held high. He even promised me that he wouldn't let anyone make him feel like he didn't belong there. I should hope so, it's his business after all, literally.

Me, I'm back at the Center today. It's one place in my life where I feel safe, useful, and valued.

It's very early, and it's just Moira right now. Moira runs the place. She's in her fifties—a sturdy, big woman with a short, black, pixie haircut. I have in the past thought that Moira was not the most skilled person in the world for that job. She's not terribly compassionate; she doesn't know how to operate a computer, to the point where if she can't find a Word document, or if she can't figure out how to print something, she'll get her IT guy to come in for a cool $165 an hour. Nigel is his name. Nigel will turn on the computer, open Windows Explorer, select the document, and print it. Nice work if you can get it. But hey, why should I care? I'm not there to tell them how to run the joint, I'm just there to make the world a better place.

"My Lord, Tamra, I didn't think we'd see you today!"

I take my coat off and hang it on the rickety wooden hanger in the corner.

"Why's that, Moira?"

"Well, you know…" She lets the sentence trail, and I look at her straight on.

"Know what?"

"I saw you on TV yesterday."

"Did you?"

I take my place at the desk, and she comes and sits next to me.

"Tell me, what really happened?" she asks, her face bright with the anticipation of gossip.

"If you saw us on the TV, you already know. Some people are spreading vicious rumors about my husband, and he's standing up and defending himself."

She raises an eyebrow at me, then she nudges me with her fat elbow and smirks. "You know what they say…"

"Why don't you tell me?"

"About being no smoke without fire. Tamra, the poor girl, right near your house—"

Just as she says that, all the other staff walk in at the

same time. All four of them stop in unison when they see me, like they don't know what to say or what to do, and I realize it was a mistake coming here. What was I thinking? That we would all simply pretend nothing's happened?

I throw her my most cutting stare. "Why don't you come out and say it, Moira?"

And because she's not the brightest spark in the firmament, she takes my question at face value. She nudges her chair closer to me, even though the others are making no secret that they're listening. With her little pig eyes boring into mine, she says, "Aren't you scared? To be in the house with him?"

I stand so quickly that I make myself dizzy. I look them all in the eye, one by one. I can't make up my mind if I should go for '*should I be? Scared?*' but I quickly settle for the loyal wife angle.

"My husband is a good man. He's a kind and honest man, and if you went to our church, you'd see that. You would be embarrassed to be speaking about him like that. There's a terrible tragedy that's taken place here, and that poor girl is dead! We should all think about her and her poor parents! Can you imagine how they must feel? But to cast aspersions like that onto my husband—" and I turn to face Moira as I say this, "—is deeply, deeply unfair. There's a monster out there—" I lift my arm and with a trembling hand point at the window "—who not only has killed a young woman but is intent on hurting my family. You of all people, Moira, know what violence really looks like, and I can't believe that you would gossip like that about my family. We're in real danger, you know. We are being targeted by an evil stranger and we have no idea why, or who. But my husband is standing tall and doing everything he can to protect his family, and I'm real proud of him for that."

I finish with, "Any questions?"

You could hear a pin drop. One of the girls lifts a finger to wipe a tear, and someone claps. Moira stands and takes me in her arms, wedges me against her generous bosom, and says, "I'm sorry. Forgive me."

Then we all hug and someone says they brought donuts and someone else makes a pot of coffee in the seedy kitchenette and I feel fantastic. For a moment there, I even believed my own words.

It's that kind of day, the kind that just gets better and better. Just as I finish my work at the Center, my cell rings. I don't recognize the number, but I take the call, anyway.

"Tamra. It's Patti. From Mike Mitchell's office."

"Patti?"

"Is this a bad time? I want to apologize."

"No... Okay..." I say, not completely certain what's coming next. Her clipped tone is a little confusing, but then again Patti has never called me before, and certainly never said something so nice to me.

"I have the utmost admiration for the way you are standing by your husband. I am also disgusted by his behavior, I don't mind telling you."

"What behavior?"

"I've been reluctant to say, because it's none of my business, and I pride myself on staying out of people's affairs—"

And I wonder if she realizes how badly she just put that, but probably not, because again, Patti is not terribly self-aware.

"—but I have been aware of certain transgressions, let's say, which I've decided, you have every right to know about."

This girl talks like a dictionary. It's kind of off-putting as it requires a fair bit of concentration. "What are you saying exactly?" I ask.

"That he's been screwing around."

I knew it. I knew it was someone from work, as per usual. Why shop around when he has an office full of bright, young, lithe things right under his nose? My chest tightens, and my heart feels like it's being squeezed. And there I was, inching back in. Getting sucked into his manipulative trap.

I'm embarrassed, too, because I'm his wife and she's his secretary, and he shouldn't behave like that in front of the staff. I'm about to contradict her, 'No no, you must be mistaken, Mike assures me he's been completely loyal,' but instead I blurt out, "Who is she?"

We meet for coffee because I have to know. On the way, I console myself with the thought that Mike and The Slut are no longer an item. I know this, or I'm pretty sure I know this, because I've checked his phone incessantly, he hasn't been sneaking out lately, and the way he's been with me—well, sorry, but you can't fake that. Anyway, let's face it, it's not like he's the catch of the century. Not anymore.

Patti's already here, her lips pursed, blowing on a cup of steaming liquid that turns out to be chamomile tea. I've got butterflies in my stomach. I can't work out if it's because I'm excited to find out, or devastated.

She tells me again how impressed she is by my loyalty —again, words I never thought would come from her lips.

"You said before, that Mike's been screwing around."

She winces, looks away. "I think I'll be resigning soon because of it. I don't think I could stand to work in his office much longer."

"You don't need to do that. Keep your job. We all have to eat, Patti."

She shakes her head a little, like she's thinking about it. Wait. I forgot. Patti is one of those completely self-centered people that pretend they're overly loyal and selfless. Are we going to be here so that I can counsel her or something? Jesus.

"I was shocked to hear the news about that poor girl, Charlene," she blurts, holding onto her cup so tightly that her fingertips have gone pale.

"Of course, you worked with her, didn't you?"

"That's right."

"What was she like?" I twirl a spoon in my coffee so that I don't have to look at her. I'm hoping it makes me look nonchalant and not particularly interested.

"It's hard to remember to be honest, she wasn't with us that long."

"Oh."

Then she reaches across the table and puts her hand on my arm. I force myself not to squirm away.

"I was aware that they were having an affair, Tamra. I'm terribly sorry."

"You were?"

She screws up her eyes and nods quickly, like now that she's given in to the impulse, she can't stop.

I tentatively pat her hand. "How did you know?"

She sighs. "Unfortunately, they didn't make much of an effort to hide it."

"Unfortunately?"

She shoots me a look. "Do you think it was pleasant? Knowing what she was doing? In front of the whole office?"

And here we are again, making it all about Patti.

"Of course. That must have been very unpleasant," I say, and I'm wondering what we're talking about exactly because the way she puts it, I have visions of Mike and Charlene going at it on Patti's desk at peak hour, and it's an image I'm keen to displace.

"What did she do, exactly?"

The sharp whirr of a coffee grinder comes to life behind me, and I have to lean in to hear her.

"She would walk inside his office without even knocking sometimes, and next thing you know, he's drawn the blinds."

I feel sick. I supposed I asked, but I didn't think she was going to put it quite that bluntly.

"It went on all summer. It was disgusting." She shakes her head. So it hadn't been *just once*. It had gone on for the duration of her employment, more or less. Just as I thought. I wonder if Mike has done that the whole time we've been married: have affairs with the staff. I look away.

"I'm sorry," she quickly adds.

"That's okay."

Neither of us speak for a few minutes. We're both in our own little world, sipping our drinks. The coffee is hot and bitter on my tongue. She keeps blowing on her chamomile tea that surely must be just about tepid by now, while I'm desperately trying not to smash my cup into the wall.

I wait for her to say something about The Slut, but she's lost in her own thoughts.

"What about the new one?" I prompt, finally.

"The new one?"

"You said he's been screwing around."

"Well, yes! With Charlene! Under the circumstances. I thought you had the right to know."

"Oh!"

"Seeing you on television, how you stood by him like that, when I knew very well that he was lying, well I said to myself, 'Patti, you need to speak up. Tamra should know.'"

"I see."

"I hope I did the right thing?"

"Of course, you did. Thank you."

"Are you sure? I didn't upset you, did I?"

"No, no. It's fine."

She studies my face for a second, which annoys the crap out of me, then she says, "You didn't know, did you?"

"About Charlene? Well I—" It occurs to me she's enjoying herself while pretending she's had to wrestle with her inner demons before deciding whether to tell me or not. I'm about to say that I did know, that he confessed everything because we are a team and we are going to get through this and come out the other end stronger than ever, and it's nobody's business, but I don't.

"No. I didn't know."

"Well, I hope it's all right, that I told you. I thought you should know, you understand?"

I so don't want to be going around in circles reassuring this woman, so I cut to the chase just to get out of here. "You're saying there hasn't been someone else? Someone more recent?"

"At the office? No."

I don't know why I'm disappointed. I finish my coffee quickly and pull out my wallet.

"Thank you, I appreciate you telling me. If you don't mind, I should go."

She gives me a sad little nod and goes back to blowing softly on her chamomile tea. It occurs to me that she told me just to see my face. Because she's jealous. She saw us together on TV and she saw the way Mike looked at me, and the things he said to me, and she must have stayed up all night trying to work out if there was a way she could burst my bubble. I just want to get out of here.

Just as I leave she says, "Enjoy the fundraiser."

I turn around. "The fundraiser?"

"For Pastor Frank's church expansion project." Then she quickly puts the cup down in the saucer and looks at me like she's been slapped. "Forgive me, you and Mike probably wouldn't want to go out in public so soon. I'm so sorry. That was thoughtless."

"That's okay, I just forgot. Lots on my mind. Yeah, I'll probably go. Mike will want to go, I'm sure. He is very involved with our church, as you know." I have no idea what she's talking about, but if it's about Pastor Frank, and it's about money, then no doubt Mike does. "We'll see you there, I guess."

She shakes her head. "I'm Catholic." And with a small smile of apology she adds, "Always have been." And I offer a silent prayer of thanks.

Chapter Twenty-Two

We didn't know anything about the fundraiser. Actually, that's not true. There had been talk of a fundraiser for Frank's church, yes, but that was a while back, before the dates had been settled. When I tell Mike, he says nothing for a second, then he does that snappy thing with his neck and he says, "Looks like we're going out tonight, baby doll."

He barely utters a single word after that. But he gets changed into his beige Chinos and a white shirt, and I choose a short, sequined, revealing little number that makes men stare at my legs, church or no church.

We drive across to the Country Club that's been hired for the evening. This isn't a pass-the-plate type fundraiser. This is the VIP version, where the entry fee will set you back a cool $500 per head, and we don't have tickets. It's not like we can pay cash right here and now, and someone will stamp the back of our hands with a star. You have to be on the list, and we are not.

Mike is livid. He's already got a couple of Scotches in him, which doesn't help his anger management, I notice.

There's a young man in the foyer with an iPad and a name tag that says *Cherryhill Abundance* and underneath, *Hi, I'm Ben.*

Ben tries, he really does, but no matter how many times he checks his listing on his tablet, there's no mention of either Mike or Tamra Mitchell, and he's terribly sorry but it looks like we don't have tickets.

I'd love to go home, not because I don't enjoy a good party, but because we are embarrassingly underdressed. I can see through the double doors into the main dining room that the men are wearing tuxedos and the women are in evening gowns. Mike looks like he's dressed for a slow round of golf, and instead of feeling sexy, I just feel tacky.

There's a line forming behind us, people muttering and feet shuffling and necks craning, because there's only one Ben and one iPad. I pull at Mike's sleeve and whisper in his ear that he's making a scene, and it's not a good look under our circumstances. He looks at me with pure hatred for just a second, and I'm actually nervous.

Then out of the blue, Brad King shows up. He extends a warm handshake to Mike and slaps him on the back like with a *so great to see you buddy*, and he tells me that I look like an angel before kissing my hand. I don't look like an angel. I look like I belong on stage in Las Vegas, but I appreciate the sentiment.

Without us even noticing, he has shuffled us to the side and Ben can finally check all the real VIP's off his list as they move up in the line before piling inside the grand dining room.

"I can't believe it. What a monumental screw up," Brad says. And he looks really annoyed, too, and he says sternly, "Don't worry, Mike. I'll get to the bottom of this.

You'll be inside in a flash." Which surprises me because surely he's not in charge, is he?

Mike's lips are pale with anger, but then they twitch into a half-smile before returning to their tight line. It's like he can't decide whether to thank him or to curse at him. Brad King is another contender for state governor, so normally, Mike would barely acknowledge him. And yet here we are, and Brad King is going out of his way to get us in and make us feel good about it. Had the roles been reversed, I have no doubt that Mike would have laughed in Brad King's face before calling security to throw him out.

But instead of just ushering us inside, Brad tells us to wait right here, and that he'll be back in a sec.

I pull at Mike's sleeve and whisper in his ear, "Can we just go home?"

"Don't be ridiculous. We're here now."

People are looking at us because most of them know who Mike is, and if they didn't before, they do now. So, each time a couple passes us on their way to Salvation by Donation, they throw a disapproving glance at us. I smile apologetically at the wives who look me up and down with barely hidden disdain.

"I just don't feel good about this, Mike." But he ignores me and keeps tapping a foot on the carpeted floor, craning his neck each time the double doors open to let another real guest in.

When Frank comes out with Brad King, I finally breathe. We can just get in there and we'll find ourselves a nice dark corner and do whatever it is everyone else is doing back there. Eat, I guess.

"Mike! I'm so sorry to keep you." Frank grabs his hand and does the back-slap thing, but instead of turning around and opening the doors for us, he takes Mike by the elbow and leads him away, toward the exit.

"What are you doing here?" he says quietly.

"I'm here for the fundraiser, what else? Something's happened to my invitation by the way, so I haven't prepared anything, but I could speak off the cuff, you know me."

For a guy supposedly so smart, I can't believe that Mike still hasn't figured it out.

"No, no. You can't be here right now. Not with the scandal that's following you around."

"The scandal? There's no scandal, Frank! They're just ugly, vicious lies!" That's the power of self-belief. Right there. Mike is so convinced that he's done nothing wrong that he has erased both the affair and the pregnancy from his history. And the rest. Delete, delete, delete. There. Never happened. Even when he talks to the man who helped him get rid of the problem, so to speak, he can deny it ever happened to begin with. There's something to be admired in that, I think. Not everyone is capable of such self-delusion.

"And we're suing the papers!" he almost shouts, standing tall, like it makes it all okay, I guess.

"Mike, the police are involved now. I can't be associated with this!"

"But that's a misunderstanding!" he snaps. "We're clearing it up, aren't we, Tamra?"

I blink and nod.

"It'll blow over," he adds.

"So come back to see me when it has, all right?" Frank is looking over his shoulder now. Like he can't wait to get back to what he was doing.

"But I belong here! I'm going to be the next governor!

Remember?" There's the sound of the crowd clapping, and Mike stretches one arm in a sweeping gesture toward the dining room doors just as they open, and I catch a glimpse of Rob and Bethany Wolfe, seated in the front row, their smiling faces upturned, almost enraptured. I tug at Mike's shirt and at the same time crane my neck a little to get a better view. And there he is. Brad King, on the stage, microphone in hand, and before the doors swing closed we hear,

"...proud to announce my candidature for governor of our great state!"

I thought Mike was going to grab Pastor Frank by the lapels of his jacket and throw him against the wall. I don't think I would have tried to stop him, either. And then, in the blink of an eye, his features went from roaring enraged to—calm?

"All right. Let's go." He takes my hand in his, and we leave.

He's literally dragging me down the street to the car. I ask him to slow down. "I'm in my six-inch Louboutins, Mike!" But he doesn't hear me, or pretends not to, and all I can do is hang on for dear life. Thankfully, the car isn't that far, and I make it without flying headfirst into the sidewalk.

"It's him," he says quietly, but that's a ploy to make me relax because when I ask, "Who's him?" suddenly he's banging on the steering wheel.

"Fucking Frank. Unbelievable! What a grade-A asshole!"

"Yeah, that was rough, not letting us in like that," I say.

He snaps his head around and stares at me like he's

only just noticed I'm here. "Don't you get it? Frank's the leak!" he says.

I don't get it, but that's okay because he turns sideways to face me fully, and he explains it all to me, his faced flushed with rage.

"We gave Frank twenty grand for his church, but I'll bet my bottom dollar that Brad King more than matched it. That's why he was there that night, at the sermon. He came to sniff out the competition, then he upped the offer. Then Frank, being the greedy prick that he is, decided to take Brad King up on it." He slams his palm on the steering wheel. "I've been conned."

He stares at me, frowning, waiting for a sign that I understand what he's saying.

"Right." I say, nodding. "But also, if you don't mind me saying, Mike, you're damaged goods. That could be why he dumped you as candidate, in favor of Brad King."

Mike shakes his head, blinking quickly. "No Tamra, you don't understand. Frank leaked the story about me and Charlene, so that he would have a good excuse to walk away and take Brad King's money instead. Problem solved."

I pretend to think about it. "Okay, I can see how that works," I say.

"Damn right!" he exclaims.

But then I add, like an afterthought, "Or! To play devil's advocate here—see what I did there?—anyway, it's also possible that with Charlene turning up dead, Frank might have thought the story was a bit too hot for him to sponsor you, if that's the term here. I mean he did have some involvement with the... the intervention. And please watch the road, Mike, you're making me nervous."

Chapter Twenty-Three

Mike's only just left for work this morning, but I'm still in bed. I desperately want to catch up on some sleep. He's kept me up half the night with his rants about how he was going to get his money back, and Frank better watch himself because he knows a thing or two about what's going on in that phoney church of his. By the time I fell into a slumber, it must have been close to two am.

My phone rings. I put the pillow over my head, but then I change my mind and reach for it. I'm about to put it back on the bedside table because it's a blocked call, and in my experience that's usually either bad news or someone trying to sell me something I don't need, but then I think of Fiona Martin and she wouldn't reveal her number if she called me, so I answer.

"Tamra Mitchell speaking."

There's a short, sharp gasp at the end of the line.

"Who is this?" And I don't know if I'm imagining it, but it sounds like a woman's whisper. Or maybe someone covering the phone.

Well, well, well. And who might you be? I wonder to myself, And before I know it, I'm yelling like a mad woman.

"I know who you are. How dare you call my number? How did you get my number? Mike won't take your calls, is that it? He wants nothing to do with you anymore! Slut!"

But she hangs up on me.

I'm not going back to sleep now. I'm so angry I could scream. How dare she call me? I stare at the ceiling, going round in circles in my head trying to figure out why The Slut would call me now. Or maybe it wasn't her. I mean, she's moved on, hasn't she? Mike sure doesn't look like he's screwing around. He wouldn't have the time! And we've barely been apart those last few days.

I'm still trying to figure it out when I hear a car pulling up outside, and for a moment I think Mike's back. But then the doorbell rings, and I pull back the covers and swing my legs out of bed. I put on my robe and I'm about to enter the bathroom when Madison is at my door.

"It's the cops," she says, one naked foot resting on top of the other.

"Really? Is it about last night? The scuffle between Mike and Frank? I mean, Pastor Frank?"

"I don't know. It's the same cops that were here before."

"Well, Mike's not here, can you tell them? He's gone to work already."

"It's you they want."

Chapter Twenty-Four

I grab my yoga pants from the back of the chair and a sweatshirt and I'm dressed in a flash. My hands feel sweaty and my heart is beating too fast. I tell myself not to panic, but it doesn't quell the tightness in my chest. I quickly grab my cell and call Lauren. It goes straight to voicemail.

"Hey Lauren! Just remember if anyone asks, I was with you that night, okay?" I whisper, brightly.

When I reach the top of the stairs, I can see both O'Brien and Torres at the door, waiting silently. I take a breath and walk down as nonchalantly as I can.

"My husband isn't here right now, Detective, he's left for work already. You'll have to call him there." I'm praying that Madison got it wrong and they'll apologize for disturbing me at this early hour and then they'll go away.

"We don't need your husband, it's you we want to talk to, Mrs. Mitchell," Torres says, and my legs wobble. I desperately want to sit down, but instead I hang onto the bottom of the banister a little tighter, and stand taller, like I'm some aged movie star in a dramatic moment.

"I'm busy, Detective, so that's a no. And you heard my

husband. He doesn't like you talking to me, and I agree with him. It's not right to pit a wife against her husband, don't you think? No. You probably don't."

"Mrs. Mitchell—"

"I know my rights. You can't make me testify against my husband. Everyone knows that." I feel dizzy. I'm still hanging onto the banister, and I grip it hard for support.

"We'd love to chat all day and discuss the finer points of the law, Mrs. Mitchell, but we're not here to ask about your husband. We have questions for you, and we'd like you to come with us. Now."

My stomach turns to jelly. "Come with you where?"

"To the station, Ma'am."

I scoff. "Don't be ridiculous. I'm not going with you to the station. I suppose I can spare a few minutes if you want to talk here." I turn to indicate the living room, trying to stop my hand from shaking, and I see Madison standing a few steps behind me, biting the side of her thumb.

There's something in her eyes and when O'Brien says, "I can go and get a warrant for your arrest right now, Mrs. Mitchell, if that's what you prefer." It occurs to me that Madison is actually really frightened.

The journey is a blur. They've put me in the back of an unmarked car, thank God, because I don't think I could bear the embarrassment. I keep asking them why they need to talk to me, but all I get is, "Just wait until we get there, Mrs. Mitchell."

And now we're here, and I'm desperately trying to get a take on what's going on. When a young woman in uniform takes me to an interview room and asks if I want some water, I'm thinking that it can't be so bad then, right?

The cops don't offer drinks to hardened criminals, do they? Or is it a human rights rule or something? That no matter how bad the crime, the suspect should be offered refreshments?

I turn it down, and she tells me to take a seat and leaves the room. My heart is beating too fast. Now I wish I'd taken up her offer because my mouth is getting dry. The only sound is an annoying buzz from the fluorescent lights. There are no windows and that, along with the dark gray walls, is beginning to make me feel claustrophobic. Maybe I could tell them I don't feel well. That I need an ambulance. They'd let me go then, wouldn't they? I drum my fingers on the table. Why did they leave me here, alone in this room? I look around for a camera and sure enough, there's one in the corner, just below the ceiling. Are they watching me? I wonder what would happen if I just got up and left. Then I wonder if the door is locked. Of course not. I'm being ridiculous.

When the door finally opens, I jump. Torres and O'Brien come in, each carrying a folder, and they sit down opposite me at the table. I try to read their faces. Is it bad? I give them a quick smile and rub my palms against my thighs.

"Why did Charlene Donovan have your phone number on her?"

"Excuse me?"

"Your phone number. It was tucked in the pocket of her jeans. Can you tell us why?"

My chest hurts. It's like someone punched me in the gut and it makes me lose my breath for a second. "Are you sure it was my number?" The words come out thick and blurry, like my mouth doesn't work properly.

"We called it. Thirty minutes ago."

My head is spinning. Nothing makes sense. I didn't talk to the cops this morning, did I? I've only been up for maybe an hour, why can't I remember? Maybe I was half asleep, but I'm sure the only call I got this morning was—

"That was you?"

She nods.

Oh, God. "But why didn't you say something? Why did you hang up?"

"We called the number we found on Charlene's body. We didn't know it was yours."

I'm trying to make sense of this, but it's hurting my head. I rub two fingers on my temples. "You must have had that piece of paper for days, and you waited all this time to bring it up?"

"The paper was faded, it took a while to identify. As of this morning we know that it's your cell phone number."

I'm going to be sick.

"Why would she have your phone number, Mrs. Mitchell?"

I can't even get the words out. I shake my head.

"Mrs. Mitchell," O'Brien says. "We are trying to find out who murdered Charlene Donovan."

"I want to make a phone call."

I stand outside in the parking lot and I call Mike. He says he already knows I'm here because Madison called him. I want to ask him why he didn't get in touch right away if he already knew. There are no messages from him, no missed calls, but I don't bring it up.

"I'm scared, Mike. I'm really frightened. You've got to help me."

"It's going to be okay, babe. I promise," he says, his

voice low, almost a whisper. "I'm coming to get you, you got that?"

"They said she had my phone number on her, in her pocket," I whine. "What am I supposed to say?"

"They haven't arrested you, have they?"

"Jesus, no! Why would they arrest me?" I can't breathe. My heart is thumping in my ears. *Arrested?* "I have to tell them everything, okay? I can't hide the truth any longer, if I do, I'll—oh, God."

"So you tell them, babe. You go for it. It's time we just told the truth and then we can move on."

I close my eyes. I can feel the weight lifting off me. "You mean that?"

"You bet."

I take a deep gulp of air. It feels like the first time I've taken a proper breath since the police arrived at my house. "Thank God. You have no idea what those words mean to me."

"It'll be okay, Tamra."

"Should we call Alex Pace?"

"It's up to you. I can call him if you want me to. But it's just an informal chat, right?"

Is there such a thing as an informal chat with the police? "I don't know. I think so."

"I'm coming right over, okay?"

"Oh, Mike. Please come. I won't let you down, I swear."

"I know you won't."

"Mike?"

"Yes?"

"I won't tell them what I saw that night. I swear. You can trust me, okay?"

There's silence and for a moment I wonder if we got cut off, then he asks, "What night, baby doll?"

Twenty minutes later, I'm still sitting in the interview room by myself when O'Brien comes in with another guy I've never seen before. "This is Detective Cal Shaw, Mrs. Mitchell. He's going to take your statement."

Weirdly, all I can think of is that this guy is drop dead gorgeous. He's a lot like Mike—same build, same dark hair that falls a bit off his forehead, and he has the same gesture, too, the way he pushes it away. But Cal has blue eyes, whereas Mike has deep brown eyes. Almost black. And Cal looks like he's in his mid-thirties. Mike's fifty-two. But because I have pea soup where my brain used to be, I decide that if I flirt with this guy, he'll go easy on me, and he'll let me go.

I smile, bring both hands up to tidy up my hair.

"You're okay with that, Mrs. Mitchell?" Cal Shaw asks and I suddenly get the feeling it's the second time and they've been waiting for a reply already.

I nod quickly. "Yes, yes, absolutely." I check out his hands and feel a tingle of hope at the discovery of a clean, ring-less finger. "But only if you call me Tamra," I add, all coy. Knowing deep down that I'm really going completely crazy.

He flicks me a raised eyebrow and says, "And you can call me Detective Shaw. I note that you declined having a lawyer present."

"That's correct." Mike's right. It's just an informal chat. I have nothing to fear. Asking for a lawyer is a sign of guilt. Everyone knows that.

He explains to me that I'm here to make a statement and it's my choice. I can leave when I choose.

"I know that, it's all good," I reply.

"Can you explain to us why she had your phone number?"

"I didn't kill her."

"Okay, that's good to know." He jots something down.

Suddenly, it's too much. The stress of the last few days. The tears come in one big sob. I wipe my nose on my sleeve. "Sorry. I'm scared. I don't want to go to jail."

"Tell me what you know, Tamra," Shaw says. I notice O'Brien's quick, disapproving frown. I guess she objects to him calling me by my first name. Or maybe they're setting up a good cop / bad cop thing.

I quickly run both hands over my face. "Is Mike here?"

"Not yet."

I put the heel of my hands against my eyes and then almost in a whisper, I say, "I drove her to the abortion clinic."

I can tell from their faces that whatever they expected, it wasn't that. I tell them my story—or part of it, anyway. "I drove her there because Mike asked me to. He was paying her a whole lot of money to have this abortion. That was the deal. That's why we had to sell the house near Badin Lake. He wanted to be sure she went to the clinic at the appointed time, and only then would he transfer the money. He said he couldn't trust anyone to do it, except me. And he couldn't do it himself, for obvious reasons. So I agreed to drive her."

"Why couldn't she drive herself?" O'Brien asks.

I shrug. "I don't think she had a car." And before she asks why she wouldn't find a different mode of transportation, I say, "And he wanted to be sure she got there. He didn't want her to change her mind at the last minute. That's why he asked me. I was to pick her up and take her there."

I think back to that night, when he told me about the affair. He looked so… frightened, so fragile. He was on his knees, holding my hands. "You have to help me. I can't do this without you," he'd said. I really believed he'd been taken advantage of. That he had been weak, because she had been relentless. Because that's how she made a living. She seduced weak men then she found a way to extract money from them. That's what he said and that's what I believed. Damn right, I was going to help him.

O'Brien pushes a notepad across the table in my direction. "Can you write down the name and address of the clinic? And the exact date and time that you drove her."

I write down the details. I know them by heart of course, I already went through this with Fiona Martin.

"Did you pick her up, too?" Shaw asks.

There it is. The question I've been dreading. I don't reply right away. Instead I take my time, keep writing, pretend I have difficulties remembering all the details.

"No," I say at last. My heart beats a little faster as I wait for one of them to ask me why. *Why didn't you pick her up, Tamra? Because someone else did, that's why. And then she died.*

"Did you talk to anyone there?" O'Brien asks.

Just as I reply, "No" there's a knock at the door, and a young woman in uniform pops her head in. I'm exhausted, overcome with it. I watch O'Brien get up and they have a quiet word with each other.

"Your husband's just arrived, Mrs. Mitchell," she says.

"Oh, thank God." I put my head on my forearms for a minute, then I sit up again and say, "Can he come in? He'll corroborate. Ask him anything. He'll vouch for me. You'll see."

When he walks in, I spring out of my chair so fast it would have fallen over if it hadn't been bolted to the floor. I throw my arms around him, but he barely looks at me and gently takes hold of my shoulders, pushing me away.

"What's going on?" he asks.

"Sit down, Mr. Mitchell," O'Brien says. Reluctantly, Mike takes the only chair available and sits down next to me, but he doesn't look at me. I turn to O'Brien. "Can I speak to him alone, please?"

"You must be joking," she says.

Cal Shaw tells Mike what I just told them, reading back from his notes. Then he turns to me and asks if I agree with his summary.

"Yes," I reply quickly. I want to get it over with. I will Mike to look at me, but he won't make eye contact. I begin to get an uncomfortable feeling in the pit of my stomach.

"Can you confirm your wife's version of these events?" Shaw asks.

He does a quick flick of the head, and he says, "This is ridiculous. I'm sorry but I have no idea what she's talking about."

It's like I've been slapped. "What?" I shout, stand up.

"Tamra, if this young woman had your cell phone number on her, it has nothing to do with me."

The room shifts. Tears are prickling against the back of my eyes. "Mike, don't do this. Please! You said..."

He turns back to O'Brien. "Detectives, I have nothing more to say. As I told you, I have no idea why my wife has told you these lies about me."

Chapter Twenty-Five

I have no words. Maybe I am crazy. Mike has stood up and is buttoning his jacket. "If that'll be all…" he lets the rest of the sentence trail.

There's a bit of paper shuffling and both detectives stand. It looks like they're all leaving, except me.

"Am I under arrest?" I ask.

"We're not arresting you, Mrs. Mitchell," O'Brien replies. "But we would appreciate you staying close by. We'll want to speak with you again."

Mike and I don't speak on the way out. It would be difficult anyway, considering how fast he's walking, miles ahead of me.

I get into the car, numb with shock, and he says, through gritted teeth, "I wish you'd waited until I got there. We could have discussed it first, how to approach it."

I look at his face. The bags under his eyes. He's aged so much over the last few days. He has become a hollow version of himself. But he won't look at me. He just starts the car and we sit, completely silent, while I bite the skin around my fingernails.

"How could you?" I ask, at last.

"You need to learn to keep your mouth shut, Tamra." His jaw is almost trembling with anger. Fiona Martin's words come back to me. *Be careful, Tamra. Watch out for him.*

I turn my head towards him, slowly, deliberately. "A dead woman connected to you has been found with *my* phone number in her jeans' pocket. If I'd kept my mouth shut, they'd arrest me. And we agreed. You said to tell them the truth!"

There's a crack of lightning, and suddenly the rain that has been threatening all day arrives, heavy and fast, big drops pounding on the windscreen and with it, the feeling of having been wrong, and done wrong, and being wrong, is replaced by a sense of outrage so overwhelming that I can barely breathe.

He bites the inside of his mouth, distorting one side of his face. We turn into our driveway, the tires crunching on the gravel. He stops the car outside the house but neither of us make a move to get out. The rain stops as suddenly as it came, one of those flash storms with more bark than bite.

Should I be scared of him? Should I even go inside with him? But then, without looking at me, he murmurs, "I panicked."

"What?"

He leans back against the seat and closes his eyes.

"Before I went to get you, I called Alex Pace. He advised strongly not to say anything. But I still wanted to tell the truth, I really did, but then, Christ, being there with the cops, seeing you, I panicked."

"You panicked?" I shout. "What about me! Where does that leave me!" I grab the fabric of his sleeve with both hands and shake him as hard as I can. He barely moves, and I can't breathe. The breath won't go in. I take a great big gulp of air and let go of him. I rub the tears off my cheeks with the back of my hand. "I'm screwed."

He turns to me, his eyes pleading and swimming in tears. "I'll make it up to you, I swear, Tamra. It will be alright, you'll see."

"I covered for you." All the fight has gone out of me.

"I know you did. And I'm grateful for that. But we've discussed this a hundred times, Tamra. I made a mistake —" he holds up his forefinger, to press the point, "—one mistake, one night, that already could cost me my career. If the police find out that we paid her hush-money to have an abortion, it's going to make me the prime suspect, don't you see? I could go to jail!" He says this last bit with a wail almost, and I can no longer look at him. He disgusts me, with his self-pity and complete lack of contrition. Because of *his* 'one mistake', I am a suspect in her murder, our lives had been upended, and all he can think of is his stupid career.

"It wasn't one night, Mike. I know you keep saying that and you probably believe it by now, but you screwed that girl all summer, and I know it. You know how I know? Patti told me. And after all that, you're still going to leave me for some piece of ass. Because of you, this girl is dead, and still I covered for you. Yes Mike, I saw you. And you know what? I still helped you. I could have gone to the cops and told them what you did. You would have been in jail by now, if it wasn't for me. And you're going to throw me under the bus because you decided to run for governor and you thought this one mistake, as you call it, would not be a good look. Understandably, since your entire campaign platform is based on some vague ideal of family values which you wouldn't know the first thing about."

I am standing outside of the car, now, ready to slam the door. He leans across the seat and looks up at me, and says, "What did you just say?"

His face is white, and his lips twitch as his whole face tenses up with anger. I bend down so I can look at him square in the face.

"You heard me."

"Oh, wow, babe. You're crazy, you know that? You're really crazy." He gets out of the car door and slams the door shut. He turns away from me, waving his hands in the air. "You're nuts. I don't want to talk to you."

"Oh really? How very convenient!"

"Don't talk to me," he shouts. "Get the hell away from me! You... You're threatening me?"

"I didn't threaten you," I shout back. "I stood up for you. I'm the one—"

"You implied it!" he yells, cutting me off.

"Oh fuck off, Mike." He doesn't hear me; he's already inside the house. I run after him, trying to get a hold of his shirt, his arm, his leg, as he takes the steps two by two, and just as we get to our bedroom, the door slams in my face, then bounces open again so hard the doorknob hits the wall.

"You're angry with me?" I yell, incredulous, my voice shaking with outrage, my entire body trembling with rage.

"Enough! I don't want to talk about it anymore!" he hisses in my face.

I'm livid with anger. "You need to tell them, you got that? You can't leave things like this and have me take the fall."

"I just can't, okay? You started this, you told the cops, you have to deal with the consequences."

He looks at me with such fury, it stops me in my tracks.

"Things are going to get real wrong for me unless you tell them," I plead. "Just tell them how she was, how she lured you into a trap. It wasn't your fault. You said so yourself. They'll understand, you'll see. I won't tell anyone about what you did to her after that. I swear." The way he stares at me, it's like he doesn't know who I am.

"Are you completely out of your mind?" He opens the door and stands on the landing for just a second, turns to me, and says, "I don't even know you anymore." And I could swear he is frightened. He runs down the stairs so fast that by the time I come to the landing he's already slammed the front door.

In one stride I am back inside my bedroom, and with one hand on the doorknob, I pull the door. As it shuts I glance at Madison's room, just in time to see her door close slowly, just an inch. Just enough to be in a front row seat.

Chapter Twenty-Six

I dream I'm lying on a lounge chair next to a swimming pool. The sun is hot on my skin. The water, blue and sparkling, is beckoning. We're all laughing; it's a party. Mike's there, and I recognize O'Brien and Torres—they're off to the side playing with a multi-colored beach ball. *That's nice,* I think. *They work so hard, those two, I'm glad they're having a break.*

Moira from the Center is sitting on a plastic chair next to Patti. Patti looks nice today, much nicer than usual. She's got retro sunglasses on, the cat-eye style ones with a tortoiseshell rim, and a red polka dot bikini. They're chatting away, the two of them, sipping from straws in tall cocktail glasses with little umbrellas sticking out.

I dive in, and the water is soft and cool. Everything sparkles around me. The small bubbles of water engulf me, and it feels wonderful. But then I see her—the little girl. She's struggling down at the bottom of the pool because her hand is caught in some kind of outlet. She's panicking, her long blond hair fanning out all around her and at first, I can't get a grasp of her. Then I see her face and it's not a little girl anymore, it's Charlene. She looks up at me, pleading, she's scared. I manage to pull her out, and I look up to see all the faces looking down, distorted through the water. Charlene emerges, and many hands reach down to pull her out. Everyone is happy, and I want to come up, too, but now my hand is caught. I try to dislodge it, but it's stuck. I look up, moving my free arm so they'll see me but no one's looking. I'm going to drown, and everyone has moved on.

I wake with a gasp, my heart beating too fast and it takes a moment to breathe free of the dream.

I did want to save Charlene, just for a moment, that night. That's why I gave her my phone number. I'm a sucker for misery. Show me an abandoned pet, even a *photo* of an abandoned pet, and I'll be making plans to turn my house into a dog rescue paradise. But my feelings of empathy never last very long, since I am fundamentally a very selfish person, and they didn't last that night, either.

Know thyself, my mother used to say. I thought she was talking about me back then, but no. She was telling me that she was getting to know *herself*. And that person she was getting to know was itching to leave it all behind and trade her husband and children for a life of barefoot globe-trotting. A kind of life-begins-at-forty revelation, and a realization that it doesn't have to include anyone else.

I was twelve years old, my brother Ben was eleven. Our dad fell apart and I kept our little broken family together as I drew upon resources that a girl my age should never have to. I became the cook, the housekeeper, the strong one. I consoled my brother as he sobbed and gasped each night into a pillow wet with tears. Every day I helped with his homework, and when our dad stumbled home drunk from the bar, I hauled him to the sofa and left two aspirins on the coffee table for the morning.

I stopped going to school, and for a while nobody noticed. I was sick of the pitying stares of my classmates. No one wanted to hang out with me, because nobody likes a loser. Much later, when social services showed up on our doorstep, I made my dad say that I was home-schooled now, and everyone let out a sigh of relief.

My dad's dead now, and I can't say I miss him. I have no idea where Ben is. He was eighteen when they came to repossess the house after dad died.

"I've got myself a scholarship," he said. "I'm leaving as soon as I can."

"Where to?" I asked, confusion clouding my brain.

"Colorado." He wouldn't look at me. He stared at the ground, his hands closed into fists deep in his pockets.

"What about me?"

"Sorry," he said, and shrugged.

I haven't seen him since. I didn't invite him to my wedding, I wouldn't have known how to reach him anyway, but even if I had, I wouldn't have wanted him there. He would have stuck out like a dark cloud over my joy.

All of that to say that I know a thing or two about abandonment, and when I catch the pain of it in some-one's eyes, I can't help it. I reach out to pull them out of the sea of grief. Someone has to.

Mike and I had agreed that I shouldn't tell Charlene I was his wife. We'd never met before, and that would have been too much for both of us, I think. But I did expect to meet a gloating, cynical young woman, hardened certainly, because you don't run a scam like that without shedding some skin and joy along the way. But instead I found myself staring at a teary, slightly frightened young woman barely out of her teenage years.

Mike had warned me. "Don't speak to her. Just drive her, and don't engage. You have no idea how good she is. She will lie and twist her way into your heart if you let her." I scoffed at the time, because we were talking about the floozy who fucked my husband, right? If she wanted to get into my heart, she'd have to hacksaw her way in. And yet here I was, feeling sorry for her. And why wouldn't I? She was so young. She looked nothing like the calculating con artist who snared married men into her evil web.

She sat quietly in the passenger seat as I drove to the clinic. It was dark at that time of the evening. In spite of Fiona's questionable investigative skills, it was true that the doctor had agreed to perform the abortion without keeping records, for a substantial fee. My instructions were to bring her in at nine pm, after everyone had left. We drove for thirty minutes in silence, save for the sound of her sniffles. I leaned across her to the glove compartment and pulled a small packet of tissues.

"Here." I handed it to her. She took it from me, thanked me in a small voice, and wiped her eyes and nose.

"It'll be over soon," I said, ignoring Mike's voice in my head. *Don't talk to her. She'll trick you, just don't engage.*

"I know," she replied in a shaking voice. Then she asked, "Do you know him?"

"Mike?"

"Yes."

"Sort of," I said, noncommittally.

She let out a long sigh and leaned back against the headrest, her eyes closed. "I thought we would be together," she murmured. "I thought that's what he wanted, a future together," she added, her voice breaking.

I wanted to tell her that one night of passion does not make a future, but then I realized that's not true. It did for her. After all, she was carrying his child. You don't get much more of a future than that. I squeezed the steering wheel until my knuckles turned white. This girl, this *kid*, next to me, couldn't be more than twenty. How could he? It was one thing to let his dick do the thinking, but there were lives at stake here. Her unborn child, for one. This girl's life was going to be affected for months, maybe years to come.

"He is married, you know," I said, although not unkindly.

"I know," she replied, still with her eyes closed. I was about to ask why she thought sleeping with married men was ever going to end well, but I stopped myself. Why twist the knife, so to speak. But then she spoke.

"He doesn't love her. His wife. He says they have nothing in common. He says she bores him."

I felt like I'd been slapped. I gasped and quickly turned to see if she'd noticed, but she was still staring ahead. I felt my heart shatter in a million pieces.

Did he really say that? What else did he say? The lying, cheating, two-faced piece of dog shit, I wanted to ask. Instead I bit my lip until I drew blood.

I saw myself in my mind's eye grabbing his two-timing throat and squeezing, and I kept that image in focus until I'd managed to calm down.

"You're going home soon?" I asked, eager to change the conversation.

She nodded. "I go back Tuesday." Two days hence.

The clinic was like a large, one-level house with a porch

and a wraparound veranda. It sat in the middle of a secluded park, with lawns and trees providing some kind of privacy, and surrounded by a parking lot. I pulled up and parked right around the corner of the entrance.

She opened the passenger door and gave me a small smile. "Thank you," she said.

"What for?"

"For these." She lifted the packet of tissues to show me before placing it in her shoulder bag.

"Wait," I blurted. I grabbed the pen that had been rolling around the dashboard and found an old, faded receipt in the space next to the handbrake. I scribbled my cell number and handed it to her. "If you ever need to talk."

She took it from me, smiled, and slipped it into the front pocket of her jeans.

"Thanks, Mrs. M," she said, giving a small sob. As she turned away her face became briefly lit by the street lamp and I caught her unguarded expression. Her lips were twisted into a sneer. It wasn't a sob, that noise she'd just made, it was a contemptuous scoff.

I sat there, watching her back recede, my heart thumping as I tried to process what had just happened. Mrs. M, she called me. She knew all along exactly who I was.

I felt the tingling of humiliation spread over my face.

Chapter Twenty-Seven

I don't know where Mike went last night—I can only guess —or if he's coming back, but I can't stay here anymore. I have this terrible fear that I'm standing on the edge of insanity. I pack a bag, randomly. I have no idea what to take because my brain doesn't work anymore. It's broken, just like my heart.

The suitcase is opened on the bed and I grab a handful of things from my underwear drawer. Then I shove a couple of dresses, a pair of jeans, some shirts, whatever, who cares what I'll wear? I'll probably end up in jail, anyway. Maybe I should buy myself an orange jumpsuit, just to get used to it.

"Where are you going?" Madison asks from the doorway. She has purple rings under her eyes. It makes her look so young.

"You're okay?" I ask. She shrugs. I sit on the side of the bed and pat the space next to me. "Can we have a chat?" I ask.

When she comes to my side in small steps, I can't help it—my heart soars a little. I want to put my arm around her shoulders, but I don't dare. She's like a frightened bird that's ready to fly away at the first shudder of fear. She pulls at the sleeves of her shirt, so that her hands—or at least her wrists—are hidden. It occurs to me with a shock that she doesn't want me to see them. What if she's cutting herself? There's water in her eyes and my heart breaks for her.

"I'm going to stay with Lauren for a bit."

She nods. "How long?"

"I don't know, just a few days I hope."

"Okay."

"Madison, I need to say something to you, and I know this won't be easy to hear."

She looks up at me again, expectant, and I lose my nerve. What was I going to say, anyway, *you need to eat?*

"You can talk to me, if you ever want to. We are more alike than you realize." I smile. She gives that little nod of hers again, eyes cast down. She seems more like twelve right now. An image of Mike and Charlene pops into my head, and a sudden wave of anger rises up in me. Has Mike ever considered what his actions are doing to Madison? Of course not. No wonder the kid is messed up.

"You can come and visit me at Lauren's anytime you like. You could even stay over if you want. I'm sure she wouldn't mind."

She nods, then quickly wipes a tear from her cheek.

"Why are you so upset?" I ask.

She sniffles. "Dad said the police questioned you about that girl's death, is it true?"

Oh, thanks a lot, Mike!

"I'm just helping them, that's all."

"Is it true that Dad had an affair with that girl? That

she was pregnant with his baby. He says it's not true, that it's all politics."

I don't know what to say to that, so I don't say anything.

"Why *did* the police want to talk to you?" she asks, picking at the edges of her nails.

I take a breath. "They're investigating Charlene's death. They thought I might know something."

She looks up from under purple eyelids that look bruised with tears. "Did you kill that girl?" she asks. Her bottom lip trembles.

It's like a punch in the gut. "No! My God! No, absolutely not! You believe me, don't you?" It doesn't escape me that I sound just like Mike.

She fiddles with her sleeves and pulls out a small folded square of paper. She unfolds it, smooths out its creases, and hands it me. It's some kind of cheap flyer, like the ones you might see around the place for a missing pet. There's a grainy photo of me, taken at a particularly bad angle. I'm laughing, but in a way that makes me look demented.

Above it, a screaming bold headline makes my stomach lurch.

Tamra Mitchell is a Killer!!

Chapter Twenty-Eight

I press my palm on the bed to steady myself as the room tilts and the words swim in front of my eyes.

"Where did you get this?" I ask, my voice like a whisper.

"They're everywhere."

I snap around to stare at her. Her eyes are still downcast.

"Everywhere?" I feel dizzy. I can't breathe.

"I picked it up in town this morning. They've got them up on trees, on bus stops, even in some shop windows."

Oh, God.

I look again at the flyer and read the rest.

Tamra Mitchell killed Charlene Donovan because she had an affair with her husband, then she buried her in the woods. The police won't do anything to her because OF WHO SHE'S MARRIED TO!! Don't let her GET AWAY WITH MURDER!!!

I drop my head into my hands.

"I took down as many as I could," she says.

"You did?"

She nods. I stare at the picture. It dawns on me where this was taken. It was at Lauren's birthday party, last year.

"Are you and my dad okay?" she asks now, as if somehow, that was more important than me being branded a killer for everyone to see.

I move my hand and very gently lay it on her forearm. I feel the muscle twitch beneath the fabric, and she pulls the sleeve over her hand again, moving mine away in the process.

"I don't know," I say, that being the understatement of the century. Did he do this? I stare at the flyer again. My heart is pounding in my chest. *I think your dad is setting me up to take the fall for a murder he committed, so yeah, we've got problems, I thought we could use some personal space, you know, to think things through, see whether there's anything here worth salvaging.*

"What are you going to do?" she asks.

"I wish I knew."

She nods, then she stands and makes her way to the door. I want to stop her. I have this urge to ask her to hug me.

"Thank you, Madison, for taking these down," I say, holding up the flyer.

"I probably didn't get them all."

"I know. But it means a lot."

"That's okay, do you know who did that?" she asks.

"Not yet."

Then it comes to me. It's The Slut. *She* did this. I bet Mike stayed with her last night. I bet he told her all about the police interview. Maybe she knows what he's done, and they're conspiring to nail this on me. It would be perfect for them if I were to take the fall for this murder.

We're in a cafe, Fiona and I, close by this time, and I don't care who sees us. Fiona Martin might just be my lifeline at this point, and since I have no idea who to trust anymore, I called her.

"You look like shit," she says as she sits down.

"Thanks so much. I needed that."

She reaches down to her bag and pulls what I see is the same flyer Madison showed me earlier.

"Oh, that's great. Where did you find this?"

She lays it down on the table. "At work. Someone left a handful in the lobby. You've seen it?"

"Yes, I have, so you can put that away, thanks. I don't need to stare at it." I drove around on the way here, looking everywhere for them. I didn't see any. I was hoping it wasn't as bad as I thought.

"Can you find out where they came from?" I ask.

She shrugs. "Could be anyone. I don't know…"

"You have to help me clear my name. The cops interviewed me yesterday. Because—"

"Yeah, I heard, she had your cell phone number in her pocket."

"How did you know that?"

She cocks her head at me.

"Okay. Whatever. He's framing me, Fiona, don't you see? I'm trying to expose the truth here, and he's turning it around against me."

"Is he?"

"Yes!"

She nods, like she's thinking about what I just said. What does that mean? Doesn't she believe me?

"Okay, so what do you want me to do about it?"

"Jeez, I don't know. I was thinking a bit of investigative journalism? Ever heard of that?"

She narrows her eyes at me in a way that makes me feel like I may have crossed a line.

"Fiona, he did it. I know he did. Mike killed her, and now he's going to try to frame me. You have to help me. You have to expose him! Somebody must know something. Did you talk to Pastor Frank? He'll know who the doctor is—"

"How do you *know* your husband killed her?"

"I—" I stop, my eyes pleading. *Just believe me*, I want to say. I want to tell her but I can't. If I do, I'll have to explain how I came to be there, and then she'll want to know why I never told anyone that Mike had run over this girl.

Then I'll have to tell her what *I* did.

"I found him, your doctor," she says.

"You did?" I shout, almost bouncing in my seat.

"I should say, he found me. He saw the article and called me."

"When?"

"Last night."

"So why didn't you tell me?" I ask.

She looks at me, cocks her head. "Why should I? I'm not working for you, last I checked, you're not paying me, are you?"

I blink, then I wave a hand in the air in a gesture indicating that I don't have time for this. "So, what did he say?"

"That a woman called, and made an appointment, said he had been recommended for his discretion. He only knew her first name. He couldn't remember it but when I mentioned you, he said that could be it. Anyway, the dates matched."

I slap my palms on the table. "Well, that's great, that's fantastic. You have to tell the cops!"

"Why?"

"What do you mean, why? My story checks out! It shows I was telling the truth!"

"There's a bit more to it."

"What is it?"

"The same woman called again, that same day, and canceled the appointment."

"That's bullshit."

"That's what he said. The appointment was canceled, and Charlene never showed up. Apparently, this extra special service out of hours is something he did himself for an extra couple of bucks. He's never had any issues before. But now that it's front page news, he's worried that he'll be blamed for something he never did in the first place."

I bury my face in my hands.

"Did you cancel the appointment, Tamra?"

I shake my head.

"Did you know she never showed up?"

I don't answer.

"Tamra?"

I sit up, take a breath. "Yes."

She drops her spoon on the table and it clatters against the saucer. She's leaned back against the back of the chair and from the look on her face, she's going to walk out any minute. "What the fuck, Tamra?"

"I never canceled the appointment, okay? That's the truth. I drove her there and dropped her off, that's also the truth. That's what I wanted to tell you, and I'm sorry I didn't tell you before, but I thought the cops would put two and two together and arrest Mike. Now, it looks like I'm the one who's going to get arrested."

I've already told Fiona that I drove Charlene to the

clinic, but now I tell her the rest of it. I do my best to explain to her the fury that came over me, when I realized I'd been treated so shabbily. "I felt sorry for her, I really did. And all the time she was laughing at me!"

I'd pulled away, and I was driving back the way we came. She had already disappeared down the path and around the corner of the building, but I couldn't bear to let her go without giving her a piece of my mind. I wanted my phone number back, and the tissues, too. And I wanted to tell her that we knew exactly what we were dealing with: a piece of trash. I reversed quickly, like a mad woman, and skidded around the corner, which meant taking the road away from the main building and around a grassy knoll. And just as I got close to the other side of the building, I saw her lean towards the passenger window of a car idling outside the main entrance. She said a few words to the driver, smiled, and seconds later she opened the door and got in.

I'll never forget the shock when I realized I knew that car. It was like I'd been punched in the gut. I was staring at Mike's car. And that was Mike, driving Mike's car.

"And here we are," I say.

"Why didn't you tell me all this before?"

"I'm sorry."

"That's not what I asked." She leans forward, arms crossed on the table. "Did Mike kill Charlene?"

I knew that was coming. I look around quickly, to check if anyone's eavesdropping on us. "It wasn't like that."

"What does that mean?" When I don't reply she adds, "Do you know how this looks?"

"Actually, Fiona, I don't. I did not cancel that appointment, so I'm confused. How does this look?"

"It looks like you dreamt up this whole charade about an abortion, just so you could get her in your car. What did you do with her after that, Tamra?"

"For fuck's sake, that's ridiculous."

"Is it?"

"I just told you! Mike picked her up in his car. I saw them! He's the one you should talk to!"

"Don't think I haven't tried."

I lean forward and reach for her arm. "You have to help me clear my name, Fiona," I whisper, my tone urgent. I can hear how desperate I sound.

She snatches her arm away. "Let's get one thing straight, I don't have to do anything, you got that?"

I just ignore her. "You need to show that he lied to the police. He contradicted me, in front of the cops! I'll tell you who can corroborate my story. Go and talk to Patti, his P.A. She'll tell you about the affair, and about the way he treated Charlene. She knew all about it at the time."

"Okay." She scribbles something. "What about Madison?"

I hesitate. "She's pretty fragile at the moment. I don't know if it's such a good idea."

"Does she know anything?"

"I don't think so."

"Okay, I might try, anyway—"

"Just be gentle, okay? Don't make her feel bad about her dad, she's in awe of him."

"I'll tread lightly, I promise."

"And Pastor Frank."

"He won't talk to me. Believe me, I've tried."

"Yeah, well, of course he wouldn't admit to anything. He's a man of the cloth."

"I wouldn't go that far," she says.

I almost laugh. "You know what I mean."

"Indeed, I do."

We both sit in silence for a while—she, twirling her spoon into her coffee, not a care in the world, me biting my fingernails till my fingers bleed.

"Do it," I say. "Talk to everyone. Everyone you possibly can."

"You understand how this looks, don't you? You know the risks?" She makes a show of counting on her fingers. "You're the last person to see her alive. She was in your car—"

"I explained about that."

"—you say you dropped her off but all we have is the word of the doctor who says you canceled. Essentially, what we have here is: she was with you, then she was dead."

I have made a complete mess of everything. "I've told you everything that I know. It's Mike you need to go after."

"So you keep saying. But I'll be writing up about the cops taking you in for questioning. It's not exactly secret information."

"Do you really have to?"

"Are you messing with me?" Her face is closed, hard. Her eyes squinting, boring into mine. It's clear that Fiona Martin does not trust me one bit.

"No," I reply.

"If I find out you've been using me—"

"I haven't!"

"Because I told you already. I'm on thin ice. I'm not writing up this story again, unless you let me write about the cops bringing you in, and why. You can't cherry-pick your way through this one. If you let me into your life, I can't guarantee what will come out. You got that?"

I take a deep breath, and before I have time to think it through, the words tumble out, fearless and bold, and I already have the bitter taste of regret on my tongue.

"I have nothing to hide. Do your worst."

Chapter Twenty-Nine

I didn't see Mike for three days after that horrible night. Which had been the original plan—for Mike to go to a seminar over in D.C. so I wasn't concerned on that score.

When he came home, he held me close, he kissed me and whispered in my ear that he had never loved anyone as much as he loved me. That I had stood by him through this showed that nothing could ever tear us apart. He'd never known anyone as loyal as me and he would never let me down. I felt his tears on my cheeks as they merged with my own, and I didn't want it to stop. I never wanted this to stop.

At first, he was so unconcerned, so confident, so relieved, that I just didn't know how to broach it. But it was odd, this lack of anxiety. Having killed her, he must have had a plan—what to do with her body? He must have gone back to where he thought she lay and found that she wasn't there. I don't think I would've been able to sleep again, not ever, if that had been me, struggling with these unanswered questions. I wondered if he saw me, saw what I did, and that's why he wasn't worried. But he never said.

And neither did I.

I didn't tell him that I saw what he did, and I didn't tell him that I drove around, in shock, until I couldn't anymore, and I stopped, I can't remember where exactly, somewhere overlooking water. The reservoir, probably. I sobbed in my car for what felt like hours, then when I'd pulled myself together, I went back, partly because I didn't know if I'd imagined the whole scene anymore.

When I got to the spot where it happened, I felt incredible relief because there was nothing. No police, no lurkers, no indication that anything had happened here. I stepped out of the car and into the chilly air and looked around. It was beautiful. The rain had left behind droplets on the trees that now shimmered in the moonlight. It was like stepping into another reality. Nothing had happened, they weren't running away together, Mike was never here and Charlene wasn't hurt.

And then I saw it.

A black shoe sticking out of the shrub, and my heart felt cold. I wrapped my coat around me tighter, and I went to have a closer look. And there she was, barely hidden by leaves and branches. I managed to turn around just before I threw up all over the road.

Did he mean to hide her? He must have but he did a pretty shit job of it. Did he mean to kill her? Why else drive her all the way out here?

I sat in my car, shaking, and to this day, I'm not sure why I did what I did. Actually, that's not true. I wanted to protect him. Or that's what I told myself afterwards. For a long time afterwards in fact. But I know now, that I wanted to protect what *I* had. I didn't want to give it up. My marriage, this life, my place in it.

Our old, empty house was only a few miles away, so I

drove over, my mind blank. I had one purpose, and one purpose only. When I got there, I thought how ironic it was. This house had been our shield against Charlene, in a way. We sold it to get her fucking fuck-money. Now it was helping us again. There's poetry in karma, I thought, as I went to the garden shed and found our old tools.

Then I drove back to where she lay and dragged her farther away, and then I dug her grave.

Chapter Thirty

I'm in the hair salon, bits of aluminum foil sticking out from my hair, and I'm flicking through recent texts and emails, thinking how kind people are. My friends and neighbors are missing me. They want to know if I'm okay. They're inviting me to things, block parties and book groups. It's my old life and I am missed.

My heart is glowing with gratitude, and that's when I get her text. It's a link. No words, nothing. Just a URL. I click on it, a little nervous, sure, but excited. I sit up in anticipation, and then I read it.

Fucking Fiona Martin.

EXCLUSIVE: New Twists in Charlene Donovan's Murder

By Fiona Martin

Mike Mitchell is a lucky man. Not just because of his good looks and healthy bank balance, but because his wife, Tamra Mitchell, seventeen years his junior, was prepared to drive Mike Mitchell's mistress to the clinic where Charlene was to undergo an abortion. You don't come across marital devotion like that every day.

We can report that three days ago, North Carolina detectives brought in Mrs. Mitchell for questioning on her role in Charlene Donovan's murder. This paper does not suggest that Mrs. Mitchell was in any way involved in the crime against Ms. Donovan, but at this stage of the investigation, the last confirmed person to see Charlene Donovan alive is Mrs. Mitchell.

I feel lightheaded. I can barely breathe. She sure went for the jugular there, Ms. *Fucking* Fiona Martin. She could at least have said that I *offered* that information, *voluntarily*. It's not like she got it as a result of her incredible investigative powers.

Tamra and Mike Mitchell have been married for six years. Only four years after their wedding did the unfortunate affair occur between Ms. Donovan and Mr. Mitchell. How did she really feel about the situation? At this early stage of their marriage? We asked the people who know her best:

'I've never met someone as jealous and vindictive as her,' Patti Huntingon, Mr. Mitchell's personal assistant, tells us when we caught up with her recently.

'Tamra Mitchell would literally storm my office, out of the blue, and scream at me that I was having an affair with her husband. I couldn't even repeat the language she used. But it was only two weeks ago that she came into the office when Mr. Mitchell wasn't present and accused me of "effing her husband behind her back." I have witnesses, too. She frightened me. Knowing now what happened to that poor young girl, Charlene, I can't help but wonder what Tamra Mitchell did to her. I can't sleep, just thinking that maybe I'm next. Oh, and I'd like to say on the record that Mike Mitchell has only ever been the perfect gentleman with me, in the five years I've been in his employment. But I'd say Tamra Mitchell has jealousy and anger management issues. Absolutely."

The psycho, two-faced bitch. Damn right you're next, Patti fucking Huntington. You ain't seen anger management issues yet.

The first Mrs. Mitchell also had a recent encounter with her replacement. When we caught up with Deborah Mitchell, this is what she had to say:

"She called me, just the other day, out of the blue. She told me my daughter was sick, can you believe it? That's the word she used! Sick! She even implied my daughter was spending too much time with her father. When's the last time you saw her? She asked me! Obviously, she can't stand Madison spending time with her own father. The gall of that woman, after everything she put our family through. We were a solid couple, Mike and I, until she came along. Our marriage wasn't perfect but what marriage is? We just hit a bump in the road, that's all. But she wanted him and that was that. That's the kind of woman she is. She wouldn't let anyone stand in her way."

I take my head into both hands and squeeze. I want to scream, and I bite my finger so hard it leaves a purple crescent around the knuckle. Hot tears well up and fall down my cheeks. Why does everyone hate me so much? I only ever mean to do good! And now what? I'm screwed. I only–

"You're okay, Tamra?"

I look up. It's June, my stylist. Her head is cocked to the side, her eyebrows knotted in concern. I've been breathing too loudly. I can hear it now.

"Yes?" I say, attempting a smile, my head leaning sideways, mirroring her. I need to get out of here but I have fucking foil in my hair. An image springs to my mind. It's a roasted turkey, and it's running down the street, foil wrapped around the tips of its wings and legs. Just like I do it for Thanksgiving.

"Okay then," June says, "let me know if you need anything, okay?"

"I will!" I reply, in a singsong voice.

I glance at the rest of the article with one hand over my eyes, fingers apart just enough to let the light in. I can't bear it, but I have to know.

Madison Mitchell, the twenty-one-year-old daughter of Mike and Deborah Mitchell, unwittingly added to the controversy surrounding Tamra Mitchell. When approached, she did not have much to say:

"She's okay, I guess. She must be smart, she was an accountant when my dad met her at Carrington & Denton. She's got an MBA with honors, too. Even my dad doesn't have one of those," Madison told us. For the uninitiated, an MBA is a Master of Business Administration. Our investigations have failed to find the university that awarded that degree to Mrs. Mitchell. Mrs. Mitchell describes herself as uneducated. 'I wasn't born with a silver spoon up my nostril (a reference to

illegal drugs, we believe). School of life, that's where I
got my education.'

Carrington & Denton have informed us that Mrs.
Mitchell was a receptionist at the time of her
employment. They were not aware that Mrs. Mitchell
had received an MBA.

I never meant to lie. Deep in my heart, these things I
said aren't exactly lies, they're shortcuts to my better self.
They still represent a part of me, they just happen to be
the parts that haven't manifested yet. Or ever.

A representative of the church attended by Mrs. Mitchell
did not respond to our inquiries but released the
following statement: "Mrs. Mitchell is a valued member
of our congregation and we are aghast at the news that
she has been questioned by police in relation to the
death of Charlene Donovan. We urge Mrs. Mitchell to
confess her sins and seek forgiveness."

That would be funny if it weren't so tragic. So
everyone is going to make me the scapegoat, is that it? I tell
June that I don't feel well. She's very concerned, very effi-
cient. She rinses out my hair in record time.

"You're sure you don't want to stay for your cut'n style?
Or even for a cold drink? Till you feel better?"

"I'll be okay. I'll be back for it tomorrow, June," I say,
ripping off the cape that was fastened around my neck. I
don't even pay. I just run.

Back at Lauren's house, I'm sitting on the lounge trying to
pull myself together. But I'm really scared. I could scream

from the rooftops of this town that I didn't kill Charlene Donovan, so what? No one will ever believe that now. My time of reckoning is coming.

When I call Fiona, I am doing so with the thought that I'm going to die of my own hand.

"How could you?" I sob into the phone.

"I told you, no holds barred, remember? I'm just doing my job."

"You didn't even write about her getting into Mike's car. That was the whole point, don't you see?"

"I can't write something just because you want me to. There were no witnesses. No one who can confirm what you said you saw. It wasn't his phone number in her pocket, it was yours."

"You don't know what you've done," I wail.

"Maybe I don't. And if that's the case, then you only have yourself to blame. If you know something, you need to tell the police. But using me to vent your innuendoes about your husband because of some revenge quest is not going to help you. I could have told you that and saved you the angst."

"You made me look like I killed her."

"Oh, no, you did that. For all I know, you wanted to be caught. It's starting to look a lot that way. Getting in touch with me, what was that about? A cry for help, maybe? Is there anything you want to tell me, Tamra?"

Is there anything you want to tell me, Mike?

"Shhh... there, there," Lauren whispers into my hair while I drip snot all over her breasts.

"I don't understand!" I wail. "I didn't do anything wrong! I swear!"

"I know. Shh. Everything will be all right."

I wish. I can't remember the last time I felt this wretched. "Can I stay here?" I wipe my nose with the back of my hand.

"What kind of question is that? You're already staying here."

"But now that everyone thinks I'm a murderer!"

"Is that why you called me and got me to come home? To ask me if you could still stay here?"

"And a shoulder to cry on," I say. Using my sleeve to wipe my tears. She pats me some more, tells me I can stay as long as want, assures me that everything will be all right, and I wish she'd stop saying that since it's not up to her, is it? We sit like this on her lovely flowery couch for at least an hour. That's how long it takes me to stop hiccupping like a child.

"Will you be okay, girlfriend? I really should go back to work. But I can stay if you need me," she adds quickly.

"No, it's okay," I say, using my sleeve to rub my nose. "I'm supposed to go to the Center this afternoon."

"That's great!" she brightens. She can't disguise the relief in her tone. That's what it's like with people. If you're miserable, they just want to hand you over to the next person. Like you're a teething baby being passed around at a family gathering. *There, you want to hold her? Sure, you do. Oh, go on, take her off my hands.*

I know I'm being unfair. Lauren is being a real good friend. It's not like she's having an easy time of it. Freaking Dwayne, that guy is never around. I need to talk to her about that, some day. That's what I think looking up at her. She's so stunning. Tall and thin, like a model, with her long blond hair and full lips.

"You're beautiful," I whisper.

"Awww, thanks girlfriend! Now, there's white wine in the fridge, red wine in the rack under the kitchen counter, and chocolate in the pantry. You help yourself to everything, okay? I'll see you tonight."

After she leaves, I sit there, remembering the soft quality of the sheets on my bed, the cozy duvet, the fluffy pillows…. Screw them. I've got work to do. I've got good people who rely on me.

I'm going to the Center.

Chapter Thirty-One

Lauren and Dwayne's house is a stone's throw from mine, if you're a very good thrower. Granted, like an Olympic thrower, but you get the picture. It's literally one minute by car. You could even walk if you wanted to, if you were desperate to borrow a shot of whisky or something. Maybe.

I want to check out my house. Why? I'm curious. What's happening over there? In my lovely home? Just a quick slow drive by the gate, I tell myself.

I'm driving south on Fisher Park Circle, which is my street, and as I come around the park, I see the cars from at least a hundred feet away—press, TV, cameras—it makes my heart skip a beat, but I suspect that turning around now would just bring attention to myself. *Keep driving*, I tell myself. *Pretend you haven't noticed the cameras, because of your very bad eyesight. You're just a regular person going to work. The sooner you're off of this street the better.* Why do I think that? Because I'm a fool, and a moron.

There's a car parked just before the gates of my house,

and I see the back of her head. It doesn't register that it's her; I thought she was another vulture calling herself a journalist. But just as I approach, I realize it's Patti. Our eyes meet, and hers open wide and she blares her horn so loudly it makes my heart jump. Then she pops her head out of the window and she spits at my car. If I hadn't had the window rolled up, she would have hit me.

"It's her! It's Tamra!" she shrieks, pointing a finger at me. "Baby killer! Shame on you!" Her outburst is so vitriolic, it gives me a jolt. In the next second, twenty pairs of eyes are trained on me. Then a horde of people stand in front of my car, snapping photos, shouting at me, shoving their boom-mikes against my window.

"Did you kill her, Tamra? Do you know who did?"

"What did you do?"

"Hey, Tamra! Over here!"

"Did you procure other abortions for Mike, Tamra? How many?"

"Are you part of a sex cult?"

On and on it goes. I glare at them, tap the accelerator with my foot, inch by inch I try to get out of there, but they won't let me.

"Fuck off!" I shout.

"Hey, Tamra, this way!"

I can't help it. I press my foot down, and they move away in unison, like those dancers in those old musical comedies. Except one. Fiona Martin has fallen over on the hood of my car.

Good, I think, as I press my foot on the accelerator just that little bit harder.

I didn't kill her, Fiona Martin I mean. And not because she didn't deserve it. I took pity on her and slowed down enough for her to let go of my windshield wipers and roll off. When I glanced in my rearview mirror, I saw Patti stand next to her car, scowling in her self-righteousness. *You're one sick puppy, lady*, I murmured.

I'm flooded with relief when I enter the Center. Even the smell of the place—normally it nudges at my senses, its acrid smell is disagreeable. But today, I welcome it, I relish it. I am home.

"Tamra!" Moira exclaims. She's standing in the small entranceway, her glasses dangling from their cord on her chest, her eyebrows raised.

"You look surprised! It's Thursday, right?" I shrug off my coat and quickly throw it onto the rack. She hasn't moved. Now I'm right in front of her.

"What are you doing, Moira?" I ask, a lightness in my voice, the edge of a giggle. "You're in my way!"

"We weren't expecting you. After everything—"

"Oh that, the papers you mean? Don't worry about it. It's all gossip. It's because of Mike's candidacy, you know what journalists are like," I chuckle. The Center has had plenty of interaction with the press, and not all of it helpful.

She lays a dry palm on my arm, and before she's spoken, I know what she's going to say.

Sorry.

Everybody is sorry. Mike is sorry, in his own fucked up way. Fiona is sorry, my brother Ben was sorry when he left me behind—me who could barely read, he with an education that I ensured was never interrupted. My mother was sorry, too, when she left us, when she stood at the door with her colorful striped bag while I held Ben against my chest and she mouthed, *sorry*, even though she couldn't hide the glint of excitement from her eyes.

Sorry, I don't care.

Sorry, I have my life to live.

Sorry, I don't need you anymore.

Sorry, I don't love you anymore.

Sorry I threw you under the bus.

Sorry, can you help me?

"I'm sorry," Moira says now, taking her hand back so she can wring it with the other. "But we think," she glances behind her then, "maybe it's best if you went home?"

My eyes well up; was that a question?

"Home!" I exclaim, bright as a button. "Heck, no! Quite the opposite! I want to keep busy! Get out of my way, Moira. We have work to do!" My hand is on her shoulder, ready to push her aside so I can get through, but she's not easily swayed, literally.

She resumes. "I meant we think it might be best if you don't come here anymore. Under the circumstances. With our funding about to be reviewed and all that. You understand, don't you?"

She's moved away from the doorway now, to look back at the others for support. And validation. I feel the wave of crimson rising up my face.

"Yes, of course," I stammer, too embarrassed to look at her now. I turn around and snatch my coat and leave.

I don't get far because I'm crying too much. There's a bench outside, a few feet away, and I grab the back of it and almost fall. The sadness I feel slices at my heart and it's devastating. I sit down and put my face into my hands and cry, and I can't stop. I cry all the unshed tears I've collected for all of my thirty-three years. I moan and bite my hands and tear at my hair and there's a voice next to me.

"Tamra?"

Chapter Thirty-Two

I don't know this woman. But she's smiling at me, and it's a lovely, kind, benign smile. The smile of someone who likes me, someone who is happy to see me, and it's been such a long time since that's happened that—

"Oh, my God! Joan?"

Joan? Joan who came to the Center last year, with her gray roots showing and her scuffed sleeves? Joan, who cared for a husband and brought up four children for thirty-five years? Joan, who got discarded with nothing when her (ex!) husband ran away with his secretary?

"You look amazing!" I cry out into her face. She envelops me in her arms and I'm so not used to that, I burst out crying again, this time into her bosom.

"Tamra! What's happening, dear?" We sit back down on the bench, and I can't stop staring at her. Her face is smooth and her skin is like a peach, her clothes are very, very nice.

"Oh, my God! Is this Chanel?" I ask, feeling the expensive wool with my fingers.

She takes my hand in hers and squeezes it, and her eyes are brimming with love.

Love, for me.

"I can never thank you enough, Tamra. I was at my lowest when I came here, and you listened—"

"Oh stop, it was my job." I try to take my hand back, I'm embarrassed, but she hangs on.

"No! You were there for me. You helped me far and above what you had to do. You gave me hope, and you introduced me to your lawyer friend—"

"That's right, I remember. So it worked out, hey?" I say, wiping my tears with the back of my free hand.

"Yes. It worked out. And it's all thanks to you."

I pull my hand away, finally, and flap it in the air, dismissing her gratitude; I push it away as quickly as I can.

"So thank you, Tamra." She pulls a clean handkerchief from her purse and hands it to me.

I blow my nose. "I hope you took him to the cleaners," I chuckle.

"Hank? No. I didn't want to do that, I just wanted to be the same, like I was before, that's all. We had plenty of money. He didn't need to hide it all away, there was enough to go around."

"Huh, so it was the new wife." I nod to myself.

"Hank says it was his lawyer who made him do it. He's not a strong man. That nice lawyer you put me in touch with? He spoke to Hank, and they sorted it all out. Hank even says he's relieved that I'm taken care of. Things are as they should be."

It's the nicest story I've heard in a long time, and it brings a fresh round of tears. She pats me on the arm and leans forward. "And they're having a baby! Hank and his young wife."

"Is that good?"

She winks at me. "I don't think Hank will like it after all this time. He wasn't terribly keen on changing diapers the first time around. But that's up to them. Good luck to him, I say."

"Wow, I'm so happy for you, Joan. I really am. I do like a happy ending. So what are you doing here?"

"I volunteer here, just like you! As of today, in fact! I want to help other women like you helped me."

I can't stop crying. I blow my nose into her handkerchief.

"Oh dear. What's the matter with you? Why so upset?"

"You don't read the papers?"

"Nah, I have no time for that. It's always bad news. What did I miss?"

"Oh, not much, I could be arrested for murder, maybe."

She slaps her palm on her lap. "You? Ha! I've never heard anything so ridiculous in my life! Who'd you kill?"

"I didn't kill anyone, but the police think I did."

"Oh, dear." She takes my hand again. Pat, pat. I don't take it away anymore. Then she unclasps her purse again and for a moment I think she means to give me some money and I feel myself flush with embarrassment. But instead she pulls out a small business card.

"What's this?"

"My name and number, that's all. I'm making new friends these days. Your nice lawyer friend Mario suggested I get these printed. It's a good idea, isn't it? So much easier that way."

After she's gone, I sit a little longer on the bench. I don't feel so bad anymore. There are some people who can do that—their good fortune makes you happy. It gives you hope. I turn the card between my fingers, I'm glad to have it. Call it a premonition, but I have a feeling I'll need it. Meanwhile, I brush my tears away and tell myself to *woman up*. I still have one card up my sleeve and it's time I used it.

This time, I don't get invited into Frank's (I think you can drop the Pastor now) office. Instead I am asked by Mrs. Lawson, who has worked here since forever and knows me well, to wait in the lobby. I wonder if he told her after my last visit not to take me to the office anymore. Or more likely it's because she's seen the article about me, like everyone else in Greensboro and beyond. Mrs. Lawson retreats out of the room without a smile or offers of refreshments, not even a glass of water. I wonder if I should ask for our twenty thousand bucks back.

I sit down and look towards the beautiful windows. There are three of them, side by side, rounded at the top, with the middle one being taller than the other two. They overlook the garden and it's a charming view. Very relaxing in fact, which is just as well since I find myself waiting for forty minutes. I suspect Frank hopes I'll tire of it and go away. He doesn't know I have nowhere else to go.

When he does show up, he doesn't even attempt to hide his annoyance. He gives me a brief smile and a curt "Tamra", then he sits in the other blue armchair, on the other side of the console table, and crosses his legs.

"I've come for absolution," I tell him.

The relief transforms his features, and his mouth makes a little 'O' of surprise. Then I burst out laughing.

"I was joking! Sorry! But you should see your face!"

He shakes his head, wants to say something but I wave my hand to stop him. "I've come to talk to you about this *other* article," —and I emphasize the word *other*—"I assume you've seen it?"

If he was offended by my little outburst, he doesn't let on. "What's going on, Tamra? Who is behind this—campaign of sabotage against you and Mike?"

"Mike thinks maybe you are," I tell him.

"That's just completely ridiculous! What on earth gave him that idea?"

"Because you endorsed Brad King when all this time, Mike was under the impression he was your preferred candidate. Mike thinks you changed your mind because Brad King made you a better offer—" I rub my forefinger and thumb together, the universal gesture for money— "and you used your knowledge to switch allegiance while keeping your hands clean. Something like that."

"I'm not responsible for your husband's deeds, Tamra, but I can assure you that I did not talk to the press. That would have put me in a precarious position, wouldn't you say?"

"Yes, I would. That's why I'm here."

I can see from the look on his face that he doesn't like where this is going. I lean forward a little. "I don't think your comments about me to the Tribune were terribly helpful. I mean, really? You're actually suggesting I may have something to do with her death? And that I should confess my sins? By the way, Frank, I always wondered, are you bound by the seal of confession even if it's murder?" then with a wink I add, "I'm asking for a friend."

For some reason, that makes him blush. He wants to say something, but I wave him off. "I'll stop fooling around. I really need your help, and that's why I'm here. As you can see from this morning's Tribune, I am well and truly in the cross hairs of the investigation into Charlene's death."

"I really don't see how I can help, unless maybe you'd like a character reference? I could possibly—"

I want to tell him that if he keeps this up, he'll be the one looking for character references. "Frank, the police know that I drove Charlene to the clinic—"

He rubs a hand over his eyes.

"But there's no proof that I dropped her off. As far as the police are concerned, I took her straight to the place where she … was found! It's not a big leap to conclude that I killed her. You see the problem?"

"What do you want me to do about it?" he asks.

"What do I want you to do about it? How about telling the truth, for once! It's not *me* who should be going to confession, *Pastor* Frank.

I'm almost shouting now, half standing, I'm losing control. Frank is pushing back against his chair, both hands clasping the armrests.

"Did you kill her?" he asks. I guess from my behavior right now, he thinks I'm capable of it.

"No."

His eyes flick to the door, which he has made sure is closed. Still, no doubt Mrs. Lawson will have heard me by now. I close my eyes, take a second. Then I lift my hands, palms facing out. "Sorry."

"Look, I still don't know what you want me to do." His mouth is trembling a little.

"If Mike would confirm that she was pregnant, and that he asked me to take her to the clinic, and you thought that was a good idea, then at least it would show I'd have nothing to gain by killing this poor girl."

"We've been over this before—"

"I don't think so, I wasn't about to be accused of murder back then. You have to convince him."

"I told you last time and I'm telling you again. There's nothing to be gained by bringing up the whole sordid mess."

"Except it's been brought up already, and I'm right in the middle of it."

"Look, Tamra, you're right, that I changed my mind about endorsing Mike. Not because of a better offer, but because the publicity surrounding his past sin is too much for our good folks. You don't need to be a genius to know that. It's very unfortunate. I would have loved Mike to come on this journey with us, but God had other plans, and here we are. But that is not to say that I want to see his life ruined."

"What about me?" I ask.

"What about you?"

"What if I get arrested?"

"If you didn't kill this poor girl, then you have nothing to fear. Stop worrying, please, Tamra. Everything will be fine. Just pray that they catch the man who did this."

"Is praying going to help? Because otherwise, I will have to explain your involvement, Frank. You do see that, right? I'll have to tell the truth."

He lifts his eyebrows, just a little. Something shifts in the room, and in that moment, I know what he's going to say.

"What truth, Tamra? These... issues between you and Mike, that's between the two of you. I've had no involvement whatsoever beyond receiving Mike's confession. And that, as you pointed out, is sacred."

"You did tell him about the clinic, the very *private* clinic." I make air quotes around the word.

"You must be joking. I have no knowledge of any clinic, and I certainly wouldn't advise Mike or anyone to encourage a young woman to do such a thing. Quite the opposite. What do you take me for?"

I make a show of looking toward the door, as if to make sure it's still closed, that there are no ears pointed our way, and very slowly, and softly, I say, "Frank, you must have forgotten, but you and I spoke at the time. It was your advice to Mike that I should be the one to take her there. You said it was best if Mike was not seen with her, even in the parking lot. That was the only way to guarantee anonymity. Those were your words."

"Tamra, I think it's you who must be mistaken. I have never had that conversation. Not with you, not with anyone."

Chapter Thirty-Three

Lauren's house is completely different from mine. I love my house, or I used to, back when I felt welcome there, but I love Lauren's place too. Ours is a typical North Carolinian colonial house with a beautiful large porch where I love to sit and watch the sky turn red in the evening. Lauren's house is this weird, French Tudor timbered thing with tall windows and a pointy slate roof. I always think of the Grimms' fairy tales when it comes into view.

But inside, it's all French country: flowery cushions on the fabric sofa, plush, colorful carpets and whitewashed timber walls. Just being here is like a vacation.

In the kitchen, I help myself to a Yadkin Valley Cab Sav and settle on a stool at the kitchen island. Her kitchen is all white cabinets and timber tops, over a floor of large black and white tiles, and I tell myself yet again how much I envy Lauren's good taste.

I take my glass of wine and treat myself to a private tour. I know the downstairs areas really well; I've been here often enough, but I want to check out the rest of the house. I'm sure she won't mind. If I thought she did, I wouldn't do it. In the quiet gentleness of the house, I feel safe and I begin to relax. I take my shoes off and feel the softness of the carpet under my toes.

Their bedroom is just as I remember, from the couple of times I've been in here, all plush and white and honeyed floors. Just looking at their bed makes me want to draw the drapes, jump in between the sheets, and close my eyes.

I check out the huge master bathroom, with one of those bathtubs with curly feet and gold faucets, although probably not real gold, and the walk-in closet—ha! Mine is better organized and larger, but hers has natural light—and then I go up the last level of the house, to the attic.

I've left it for last because I'm sure it's going to be the most exciting room in the house. God knows why I'm expecting a lush decor of Arabian nights and old trunks overflowing with treasures, and to say it's a disappointment would be an understatement. It's essentially a boring old attic with a carpet, an old, battered sofa, and a couple of storage boxes.

Back on the landing below, at the door of their bedroom, something tugs at my mind, and it takes me a few minutes to figure out what it is.

There's nothing of Dwayne here.

I retrace my steps and I'm back in their bedroom. His walk-in closet is locked. Is that strange? Who has a lock on their walk-in closet? Is that where men hide their secrets? The equivalent of a woman's lingerie drawer? Maybe I should have checked Mike's before I left.

While I can't check in there, there is nothing in the master bathroom that suggests Dwayne lives here. Not in the various cabinets, not the shelves, no grooming products that would belong to a man. The bedroom is more or less the same. It's easy to see which side Lauren sleeps on because her bedside table overflows with magazines and hand moisturizers and a whole lot of other knickknacks, but Dwayne's side has only a crumpled Kleenex and a couple of headache tablets.

I check the tall dresser, and it's the same. There's a framed photo of Lauren with her parents, but none of Dwayne. No matter where I look, I can't see a single trace of him.

"Hello! I'm home!" she sings out from downstairs. I rush out of the room and remember that I left my glass of wine in her bathroom. When I grab it and rush out, a little of it spills on my fingers and then onto the beige carpet in the bedroom.

"Where are you?" she shouts.

"Coming down!" I shout back. I make my way down the stairs to meet her, trying to quiet the confusion that has taken hold of me.

"I'm sorry I'm so late, I meant to be back in time to cook something for dinner, but I got sidetracked at work." Lauren slides two pizza boxes on the kitchen bar.

"Don't apologize, this is great." I grab a slice loaded with some kind of sausage and dripping with cheese. "You eat like this all the time?" I only ask because she's like a gazelle, a size minus one, all legs and no hips.

"No, but one slice isn't going to hurt, right?" she replies, nibbling at the edge of the crust. With her free hand she reaches behind her and retrieves a bottle of white wine from the fridge.

"Hey I was upstairs just now, checking out your room and I spilled just a teeny weeny little drop of red wine on your carpet. I mean, in my defense, who has light beige— what's the matter?"

She's gone pale. Her hand is still around the neck bottle, like she's frozen.

"Is something wrong?" I ask.

She shakes her head. "No. Sorry, everything's fine." But now she colors a little. She lifts the bottle in my direction in a silent question. "What about you? You're feeling better? You're okay?" she asks.

I shrug. "I wouldn't say I'm okay, but you know, I'll live." I must have imagined the awkwardness. I'm still nursing my glass of red, but what the heck. I tip my head back and drain the rest of the contents before handing it over. "And don't be shy, I'm self-medicating."

We're both silent for a minute, because we have manners and we don't speak with a mouth full, basically, then without looking at me, she says, "Any news?"

I reach for a paper napkin and wipe my mouth. "Like what?"

"Like… the police? Have they been in touch?"

"Not yet, but after that piece of tabloid trash this morning, I expect them any minute." And I do. Every time I saw a squad car today, I was sure it was for me. I even hid behind a construction dumpster and fell over a homeless guy who was sleeping. I felt so bad waking him up, I gave him fifty bucks.

"What about Mike, have you spoken to him?" she asks.

"You must be joking." I reach for my third slice of pizza. "What about Dwayne?" I ask, without looking at her.

She snaps her head up and stares at me. "What about him?" There's something in her tone that tells me something is wrong here.

"Just wondering how he is, that's all. I haven't seen him in ages."

"He's fine. He's good."

"Okay. When is he coming back?"

"Next week, I think."

"You *think*?"

"No I mean, I know, he's coming back next week. How was the Center?" she says, changing the topic. "That's where you were today, right?"

It annoys me that she won't talk to me about what's going on. I can feel something isn't right, but as usual lately, Lauren just deflects.

"I don't want to talk about it," I say, a little petulantly, because two can play that game.

"Oh, okay."

"Can I have more wine?"

She obliges me and refills her own. "What are you going to do, Tamra?"

"I don't know!" I snap. "How would I know? You don't plan for things like this to happen. I don't have an exit strategy, if that's what you're asking. I'm just waiting, going with the flow, I guess."

"How's that going to help?"

"I have no idea."

"What does Mike think?"

I roll my eyes. "I just told you, I haven't spoken to him."

"Why not?"

I lean forward on my forearms. "Trust me, Mike is not my friend here, okay? There are things you don't know."

"So tell me."

"No, I can't. Not right now."

She shrugs and gives me a small smile. "Okay."

She rubs a fingertip over the rim of her glass. It doesn't make any sound. She doesn't know how to do it. I'm about to tell her she needs to lick the tip of her finger when she says, "Why did you tell Maddie that you were an accountant?"

"That's quite a segue, *girlfriend*, why do you care?"

"Because you're my friend! And I'm trying to understand why you'd say that! Do you really have an MBA? Or did you make that up, too?"

"Has it occurred to you that maybe Madison made it up?"

Her lips form a perfect O. "Did she?"

I sigh. "No. She didn't. Not exactly. The accountant part, that was an assumption on Mike's part because that's where he met me. And he told Madison, and I never got around to, you know, disabuse them of the notion."

"I see. What about the MBA?"

"You do realize it's none of your business, right?"

"Hey, if I'm overstepping the line…"

"You're overstepping the line," I snap, slamming my glass down. Some of it spills out. Lauren turns around to retrieve a cloth, but not before I catch the hurt on her shocked face.

"I'll do it." I grab the cloth from her and take her into my arms. "I'm sorry, I really am. I'm so stressed, I don't know what I'm saying anymore."

"I know," she says. "But I'm your friend, and I need to understand. It's not unreasonable, Tamra."

"Yeah, I know." I mop the countertop and refill both our glasses.

I tell her about the MBA, that I was just being stupid and I lied to shut her up. That shocks Lauren, I can see that. Then I tell her that I do think that Madison is unwell. "So yes, I did call her mother, but not the way she makes it sound. I had no idea she hated me so much."

"Well, you broke up her marriage…"

"No, I didn't! They were already apart when I met Mike. He told me. They only stayed in the same house for the sake of the children."

She gives a sly look, like she doesn't believe me.

"Anyway, that's not the point! Madison is not well! Surely you can see it too! I found pills in her bedroom and I wanted to tell Deborah—"

"You went snooping in her bedroom?"

"It's not like that! I was looking for something. Oh, never mind, me snooping or not is not the point. I'm worried about her. You know that."

"Don't you think you're being a tad too dramatic?"

I don't answer. After a moment I stand up. I blame a long, horrible day and a headache, and tell her I'm going to bed early. But as I reach the door, I turn to look at her. She looks so sad, twirling the stem of her wine glass, her thoughts a million miles away.

"Dwayne's gone, isn't he." I don't make it sound like a question.

She nods, rubs a hand over her eyes and her mouth distorts as the tears well up in her eyes. This time I'm with her in two strides and I take her in my arms.

"What happened?"

She shakes her head. "He left me Tamra, he's gone."

"Oh Lauren, honey, why didn't you tell me?"

"Because I was embarrassed."

"With me? You must be joking. Haven't you noticed what I've been going through lately?"

She gives a small laugh, more like a snort, really. I ask her why he left but she won't say. She's not ready to talk about it, she says.

"That's okay, I understand," I tell her. I hold her, and we stay like that for a long time, both of us sad.

Then, from the corner of my eye, I spot something that looks familiar. It's at the other end of the kitchen counter. A notepad, the corners of its pale yellow pages curling a little. I've seen that page before, or one just like it.

I've got your back. Love you

Two hours later I'm lying awake, staring at the ceiling, trying to make sense of everything and generally losing my mind. I drift off to sleep just as I hear something, her voice, soft and low, like a whisper, on the other side of the door. I get up and tiptoe my way across and listen. When I hear her murmur my husband's name, I slowly turn the doorknob and open the door. Just an inch.

She's sitting on the top step of the stairs, her back to me, the phone cradled in the bend of her neck. I can't make out what she's saying from this distance, but there's an unmistakable tenderness in her voice that makes my heart burst with pain.

Chapter Thirty-Four

"How did you sleep?" she asks. She's got her back to me, making coffee. When I don't answer she turns around and raises her eyebrows at me. "Not so good, hey?"

No. Not so good. Barely at all, in fact. "I had the weirdest dream," I say, taking the steaming coffee cup that she hands me. "I dreamt you were talking to Mike on the phone."

She doesn't answer, turns back to the espresso machine. Finally, she says, "He called. He wanted to know how you are."

I snort, spraying coffee all over the table.

She turns around to face me, a look of surprise on her pretty face. "What?"

"Cut it out, Lauren. What did he really want?" *Because he would never call you*, I want to say. *He can't stand you, and you can barely stand him, isn't that right, Lauren?* And yet I heard her last night, all sweet and soft, and I stayed up all night trying to make sense of that, and I think I did.

"I just told you. He's really worried about you."

"Yeah. I bet he is. What about you, Lauren? Are you

worried about me? No, don't answer that. I know what you're going to say. Why don't you tell me why Mike really called."

"What's the matter with you? He wants to know when you're coming home. Did you get any sleep? You look awful."

I tilt my head at her. "Oh, thanks for that. How sweet! What did you tell him?"

"I didn't know, that's up to you. That's what I told him." I can tell from her tone that this conversation is grating on her nerves. Well, tough.

"Why did Dwayne move out?" I ask, cocking my head to the other side.

"You keep asking me that. I told you already, I don't want to discuss it." She turns away from me again and inserts a capsule into the Espresso machine. There's a convenient whirr of noise that makes it impossible to hear ourselves. If she thinks that's enough to distract me, she doesn't know me very well.

"Why not?" I ask, when she releases the button and silence returns.

"What it is with all the questions, Tamra? What difference does it make to you?"

"I think you're lying to me." We're not playing goody-goody anymore. My tone is sharp and means to cut.

"Do you?" she says, one hand on her hip. "Whatever you might think, Dwayne is none of your business."

"Why are you lying?"

"Oh, for fuck's sake! Just—"

"Just what? What were you going to say? Just shut up, Tamra? Is that it? Just fuck off? Why are you having sweet, loving talks with my husband in the middle of the night? If he'd called to talk to me, why didn't you come into my room last night to get me? What the fuck is going on here?" I feel myself getting worked up. I have a vision of Lauren and Mike together, sitting on the top of the stairs like I saw her last night, she with her head resting on his shoulder, he, holding her hand in his.

"How long has this been going on?" I ask. I feel the tears pricking the back of my eyes. I will myself to hold them back. I don't want to give her the satisfaction.

She's breathing hard, her nostrils flaring. She starts to say something, then stops herself, like she can't get the words out.

"What's the matter, Lauren, cat got your tongue?"

Her face is going red. It's not a pretty sight. Her lips are tight and twitching. Finally she says, "Why are you doing this?"

I step closer to her so I can look into her eyes. Her mouth twitches and she looks away.

"Because I don't trust you," I say.

She gasps. *Nicely done*, I think. She could have a career on the stage.

Just then, her cell phone rings. She shoots me a look of fury, but she snatches it and answers the call with a brusque hello, turning her back to me.

"Sorry, who is this? I see. Yes."

She turns and faces me again. Her eyes are squinty, hard, and there's a certain look in there… triumph?

"When? No. That's a mistake. I drove to Mrs. Mitchell's house that night, but she wasn't there. There was no one home. Of course, I'm sure. I will, this afternoon. Yes."

I'm almost climbing over the countertop, trying to snatch the phone from her, but it's too late. She's hung up.

"What did you just say? Was that the police?"

"I have to go to work," she says coldly. "Please don't be here when I get back."

The realization dawns on me that she held my future in her hands just now, and she threw it away. "Oh, my God, Lauren! What have you done? Did you just deny my alibi? You promised! How could you?"

"How could I? When you're being such a bitch? I'm not lying for you, Tamra. I have no idea what you've done or why you'd want me to. But you're on your own." Before I have time to come back with a cutting remark, she's thrown her coffee cup into the sink. It breaks with a crash, and rivulets of coffee slide down the outside. She strides out of the room without looking at me.

I'm so angry, I'm almost vibrating. "Lauren! Get back here!"

"Screw you!" she yells, and the front door slams so hard it makes the glass shake.

Great big tears roll down my cheeks. They gather on my chin and slide down my neck. I lean on the kitchen bar and drop my head into my hands. I stay like this, sobbing, for a long time, my breath ragged and my world crushed. I don't know what to do anymore. I don't know who to trust.

I'm going to get arrested. They're coming for me, I'm sure of it. And this time it won't be just for a little chat. I wipe my tears with the back of my hand and calm myself with deep breaths.

I have to get out of here. I can't even tell what's most upsetting, that Lauren turned on me and is ganging up with my husband, or that I'm about to get thrown in jail for murder. That's the kind of loser I am.

My cell phone rings with a number I don't recognize so I let it go to voicemail. There's no way I'm picking up a call right now.

I open all the drawers in the kitchen, all the cupboards. I'm not sure what I'm looking for, but I'll know it when I see it. The thought that those two are up to something is making me ill. I pull out piles of napkins and tablecloths, placemats and table runners. I mess up the cutlery drawers just because I can. Then I go in the living room and go through the bookshelves, the glass-fronted antique cabinet. I pull out all the drawers, and in one of them I find a small pile of those flyers with my name on them. My legs feel like jelly. My eyes hurt with the sudden welling of tears. That was Lauren?

I run upstairs and go through her dresser, and I'm about to close the drawer when something catches my eye. My stomach flips. Slowly, I reach for it and lift it so that it drops against the light.

It's a bra.

It's blue.

A lovely, cornflower blue. The kind of shade that would look lovely for the drapes in my living room.

Chapter Thirty-Five

There's a particular kind of grief that takes hold when a friendship dies. When your best friend, someone you trusted to love you, turns out to be your enemy. It's as if one of the anchors that grounds you in this world has come undone. I sure hope there's a special kind of hell for people like that.

I bite my knuckle until I draw blood and rock on my knees, the bra lying at my feet. I throw it against the mirror, and, clutching the top of the dresser, I stand, and in one gesture, I knock off all the perfumes and creams and face powders into the plush carpet. There, that should make the place stink like a brothel. Appropriate, too, I should think.

I can't bear to stay here a minute longer. I've barely unpacked so it takes no time to gather my things, and I'm outside and in my car in minutes. My hands are shaking, the tears are running down my face. I am the loneliest person in the universe. Everyone has discarded me. I am unwanted, and unloved, and I have nowhere to go.

There's a spot I know, about ten miles from here, where

I could drive the car off the road and into the river and have little chance of surviving. If the impact doesn't kill me, the water will. I wonder how long it takes to drown?

My cell phone rings again. I need to get rid of it so the police don't find me. But when I pull it out, I see that it's Fiona. Against my better judgment, I take the call.

"Did you call to gloat?" I snap. "Are you up for a Pulitzer or something? I hope you thank me in your acceptance speech."

"You knew what you were getting into, Tamra. We talked about that." She sounds like she's biting into something, like an apple.

"You told me already. What do you want?"

"I have an update to the story," she says, in between crunches.

I press the heel of my hand between my eyes to ward off the headache that's nipping at my brain. "Okay, I'll bite. What update?"

"We spoke to your husband, did you know that?"

Hearing that makes my stomach lurch. "What did he say?" What I really want to ask is, '*How bad is it?*'

"He confirmed he engaged in an affair with Charlene."

"Really?"

"Yep, and that he arranged for her to have an abortion."

I almost drop the phone. "He said that? How did you get him to admit to that?"

"We didn't, he called us and said he wanted to make a public statement. He wants us to publish this, so we are."

"You're kidding."

"You didn't know?"

I scoff. "No, I most certainly didn't. But I'll tell one thing for free: he's got an angle. There's no reason at this point for him to volunteer that information. Something must have happened. Did he say anything else?"

"That he was deeply sorry for the hurt caused. He never meant for it to go this far. But he maintains that he had nothing to do with Charlene's death."

Yeah. Right.

"You still maintain *you* had nothing to do with her death?"

"Damn right, I do."

"I figured you'd say that," she says, and sighs.

"Did you really call me to tell that? About Mike?"

"Actually…" There's a beat of silence. I imagine the cogs in her brain hard at work. "I want to show you something," she says at last.

"What's that?"

"Will you meet with me? Now?"

"You must be joking. You think I'm stupid? You're trying to set me up. You're taking me to the cops and you'll have a nice photo of my arrest. Nice try, Fiona."

"Wow, that's harsh."

"Yes, well, I'm all out of trust right now."

"If it helps, I have it on good authority that the police don't have a warrant out for you. Yet."

"Really?"

"You didn't hear from me, okay? The judge won't give them one. Apparently, he's not satisfied that there's enough for probable cause."

"What does that mean?"

"The police don't have enough actual evidence tying you to the crime. So it gives you, and anyone else, your husband included, the opportunity to produce any relevant alibis. That's what I'd do if I were you. If you went somewhere after you dropped Charlene off at the clinic, then you should contact anyone who might have seen you at that night."

I don't tell her that neither of us have an alibi for that night. He was there, and I saw him. That puts the both of us at the scene of her murder, although not together.

"The bad news however, is that they are frantically gathering evidence. It would not surprise me if they came to search your house, especially your cars. Someone drove out to dig her up the other night. There could be traces."

I pinch the bridge of my nose. "Do you know how long?"

"Hard to tell. Maybe forty-eight hours, maybe a bit longer."

Two days, this is too much. I can't deal with this. I massage my temples, as if that will help me think. "I can't meet right now, but I'll call you later and make a time."

She sighs. "Fine. But don't wait too long. If you're telling the truth about what happened that night, then what I have to show you could be the key."

"Wow, you're really going to reel me in, aren't you?"

"I sure hope so."

Then something occurs to me. It's probably stupid but hey, I'm all out of smarts. "There's something you can do for me, Fiona. How good are you at finding people?"

"Why?"

"Because I want to find someone. Why do you think, Sherlock?"

"You can start by dropping the attitude, Tamra, and we can go from there."

I close my eyes. "Forgive me for being touchy, but you wrote an article that has set me right into the frame of being a murder suspect."

"Who do you want to find?"

I tell her about Dwayne. His name, his home address. That's all I have. I don't know where he works, and I don't know his mobile number. But I want to know where he is, and I want a way to contact him.

"How is he connected to Charlene's death?" she asks.

He's not, of course. Heck, that would be one hell of a development. But I don't tell her that because if I did, she'll tell me to go to hell. "I'm not sure, call it a hunch."

"Really? In my experience, hunches end up in a wild goose chase."

"Then call it an educated hunch."

"I'll see what I can do. If you're really innocent, Tamra, as you claim, then I hope for your sake that this will prove it."

Except I'm not really innocent. I know that. I've always known that, otherwise, I could have just walked into the police station and told them what I saw.

What's the penalty for failing to report a murder? I don't know. I tried to find out. I Googled it until my eyes bled and I still don't know. I considered hiring a criminal lawyer to ask, but let's say that life moved on, and most days I could convince myself that I imagined the whole thing and it never happened. The other days I just forgot about her, and those days began to run together. But that was when I thought I was living my Happily Ever After.

Sorry baby, I really need you, you're the only one who can help me.

He doesn't even know how much I helped him.

Chapter Thirty-Six

Thank God for Joan. She must be my guardian angel, or maybe we are each other's guardian angels. I gave her a call, squeezed my eyes shut and I came right out with it. "I need a place to stay for a while," I said.

"Come on over. You can stay as long as you like." I let out a long breath of relief. I could tell she meant it, too, just from her voice. I made a mental note to tell Madison next time I see her.

You see, it's not about self-affirmations so much as being a nice person. Be nice to people, they'll be nice to you back. Humanity 101. As if.

And yet here I am, sitting in Joan's living room, a steaming mug of tea in my hand and a Golden Retriever at my feet. "You don't have to tell me anything if you don't want to," Joan says, "but are you all right?"

"Not really, but I will be," I lie. She already knows about my troubles with the police and I don't want to tell her that The Slut who was screwing my husband turned out to be my best friend. I don't want to tell her about all my problems. I want to forget about them, even just for a minute.

"What about our good friend Mario? Can he do something?"

Mario, my friend the lawyer. The one who helped Joan. I sigh. "Mario's a divorce lawyer." I almost add that he'll most certainly come in handy, but not right now.

"Oh, dear." She frowns. "Although, the law is the law, you would think. Well, let me know if you change your mind. We've become quite good friends, Mario, Karine and I."

Karine, that's right. She and I used to go to Pilates together. God, that feels like a million years ago.

"In fact, I'm going to Alexandro's wedding next weekend. Will you be coming too?"

Alexandro. Mario and Karine's oldest son. It's like getting pulled into my old life. "I—we have been invited, yes, but I'm not sure if I'll make it." They've probably rescinded that invitation by now. The local murderers don't exactly make ideal wedding guests. I suddenly get an image of that other wedding invitation, neatly addressed to *Mr. & Mrs. Mike Mitchell* from Janis Porter. I bet that one's been rescinded.

"Oh well, I hope you change your mind between now and then. Now, you make yourself at home. I need to be somewhere, but I will see you later. Max will look after you. Won't you, Maxie?"

At the sound of his name, Max wags his tail and pretty much knocks everything in its path. Then he turns his head toward me and nudges my hand for a pat.

"Thank you so much, Joan. I can't tell you what this means to me." I accompany her to the door.

"Oh, you don't need to," she replies, adjusting her

coat. "I know very well what it means." And with a smile and a squeeze of my hand, she's gone.

I'm so tired I make a beeline for the spare room, the room that's going to be mine for the next few days. I can't put my thoughts in order, so I figure I may as well sleep for an hour, and then I'll meet up with Fiona. But as I lie on top of the Damask duvet and stare at the ceiling, I find that sleep has other plans.

My phone buzzes. It's a text from Mike.

When are you coming home? I miss you. I love you. Please come home. We can sort this out.

He's scared of course. He wants me to retract everything, although why he talked to Fiona is a mystery. He has an angle, and I have no idea what it is, but I sure don't trust him. I start to type a reply. It goes something like, *Please fuck off,* but then I change my mind and cancel it. Clearly, he still doesn't know that I know about him and Lauren. What a creep. He's still trying to make me protect him. *Oh Tamra, I love you so much! You can take the fall, can't you? For the both of us? I'd do it for you! Not!*

Well, Lauren will be telling him any minute now. I left the bra hanging over the mirror on the top of the dresser. I figured since I had trashed her place, the least I could do was give her an explanation.

I lay a hand over my eyes, and my breath turns into a sob that brings with it a despair so deep it makes my whole body shake. Images of Mike and Lauren fly through my mind. All this time, for years, I thought they couldn't stand each other. Now it turns out it was just for my benefit.

I'm such a loser.

I slept for too long. When I wake up, the light that was

pouring through the blinds has dimmed to dusk. I don't know what time it is, but it must be late afternoon.

I notice the screen on my phone is lit, and I realize that's what woke me. The ping of a text. It's from Fiona Martin.

Ask me a hard one next time. He's staying at the Ballantyne.

I sit up quickly; Max's head pops up next to the bed, his brown eyes fixed on me. Next thing I know, he's jumped on the bed and is licking my face. It's the grossest thing I've ever had done to me. I feel like I should go and get a chemical peel done immediately before I start to grow warts all over my face. I do my very best to push him off the bed with a spray of "Down Max! Down boy!" and when he does hop off, if that's what you do when you're eighty pounds overweight, I get the feeling it's his decision, not mine.

"Jeez Max, pick on someone your own size next time."

After washing my face, I call Fiona back. "What's he doing at the fucking Ballantyne?"

"Well, hello, Tamra? How are you? Nice to hear from you!" There's no mistaking the sarcasm in her tone.

"If you want niceties from me, you'll have to write up that I'm innocent and you have no journalistic ethics whatsoever."

"I never wrote you were guilty, I just wrote the truth."

"Yeah, right," I snort.

"Did you call to berate me? Or do you want the info you asked for?"

"How long has he been there?" I ask. Is that even relevant? The Ballantyne is less than two hours' drive from where he and Lauren live, so it's not like he's away on business. He's moved out.

"He hasn't been completely alone, if that means anything," she says, ignoring my question.

"No way!"

"There was a woman staying with him."

"Really? Who?"

"Dunno. You didn't ask for details."

I don't know what to say. It sounds really fast for him to move on like that. Whatever her name is must have snatched him on the rebound.

"Did you say, was?"

"She's moved out, my informant tells me. And she was not pleased."

"Huh! I'll be damned."

"I've got the photos. You want to meet up?"

Her voice pulls me back. "Holy crap! Photos of those two? Even for you, that's a bit over the top."

"Heck, no. I'm not your personal sleezebag private investigator. You know where he is now, get your own dirty pictures."

"So what are you talking—"

"I want to show you. Feel like a drink?"

Chapter Thirty-Seven

I leave a note for Joan that I won't be in for dinner, just in case.

Fiona and I meet in one of those classic corner bars, nothing fancy. The kind that has dartboards on the wall and a karaoke stage. It reminds me of growing up back in Wisconsin. I hate the place. Nothing to do with Wisconsin I might add, and all to do with my upbringing.

We slide into a booth in the corner. Fiona orders a Peach Mai Tai, a weird choice, I think, and I get a glass of dry white wine.

"I don't know how you can drink that. It's like sickly sweet syrup."

She shrugs. "Since you're buying, I figured I'd get the most expensive drink on the menu."

"Ha! Very funny. Next time we're going to Starbucks." I joke, but actually, this place is a good choice, because it's quiet and dark.

She checks her cell phone, then, satisfied there's nothing on it that requires her attention, she sets it on the table, screen up. "What's the story with that guy at the Ballantyne?" she asks.

"It's personal, if you must know. I'm just trying to figure out if my friend—I mean my ex-friend—is being even more dishonest to me than I thought."

"Right. So nothing to do with the case. You lied to me, in other words."

"Yep."

"It's serious?"

"Why do you want to know everything all the time?"

She shrugs. "I'm a journalist, what do you expect?"

"Isn't it exhausting? Because it is for everyone else, you know? You're like a kid! 'Why is the sky blue? Why does it snow in winter? Why is your friend's friend at the Ballantyne? Why did the freaking chicken cross the road? Why—'"

"Jesus, Tamra! Okay! I get it! You can stop now." She picks up her phone, glances at the screen, then twirls the little pink umbrella in her drink. "Actually, I have another question."

I sigh. "Okay, let's hear it."

"Why did you contact me that first time? Really?"

I take a moment to gather my thoughts. I remind myself that I'm sitting across from a journalist who has no issues with betraying my innermost secrets. Somehow, that makes me trust her more.

"Mike is having an affair with my closest friend, and he's going to leave me. They think I don't know. Actually, scratch that. Lauren knows I know. I kinda trashed her place yesterday."

"I see, and that's the friend whose husband is staying at the Ballantyne." She's not asking a question, so I don't bother to answer. "So telling me about the affair and the abortion was to get back at your husband."

"I told you it was revenge. Can you imagine how it made me feel when I found out? I protected him back then, when he had the affair with Charlene. He asked me for help, to deal with her, and I did." I sneer at the thought. "I'm the worst idiot."

"He asked you to drive her to the clinic, because he wanted to make sure she kept the appointment, is that right?"

"That's exactly right. He didn't trust her."

She takes a sip of her drink, then curls her lips downward in a show of disgust.

I cock my head at her. "Told ya."

She smiles. It's the first time I've seen her smile. Then I see her phone light up. She grabs it quickly, then puts it back.

"Are you going to do this all night?" I ask. I'm about to make another sarcastic comment but she snaps her head up and frowns at me.

"It's my daughter, she's got a tummy ache. My mother's looking after her."

"Oh, sorry. I didn't know."

"That's okay. Why would you?"

"How old?"

"Six."

"Wow. Six years old." I smile in spite of myself. "That's got to be a nice age, hey?"

There's a softness that smooths out the frowns and lines over her face. She smiles, and I realize with a start that Fiona Martin is actually very attractive. Usually whenever I see her, her face is closed up in a scowl.

"Where's Dad?" I ask, knowing how impertinent the question is, but at this point, do I care? No.

"He's not around." She takes a sip of her drink and her lips purse together in a grimace, again. It almost makes me laugh.

"I have a question for you too," I say. "When I called the paper with my story, I expected one of your colleagues to call me back. One of the guys who write about local politics. *Candidate for governor had affair with dead girl*. I would have thought they'd jump at it. Instead I got you. No offense but you know, you don't write much, and not about local politics either."

"Is there a question in there?" she asks.

"Why you?"

"Simple. Because no one else wanted to touch it."

I take a moment to reflect on that. "It's because he's rich, isn't it. They were worried about lawsuits."

"No, it's because no one believed you. Simple as that."

"Really?"

She nods. "In our business, people call with crazy stories all the time. We have to sift through the noise."

"I see. But you believed me?"

She shrugs. "I can't afford to be incredulous. I'm not on the payroll." When she looks up at me, she must see the confusion in my face because she adds, "I don't get the good stories at the Tribune."

"Why not?"

She gives me a wry smile and points her chin toward the cell phone on the table. "I can't run off whenever a good lead presents itself. As nice as single motherhood is, it's also a bit of a ball and chain. No one wanted to follow up on your story because they thought you were a nutcase. But I had a hunch."

"In my experience, hunches usually lead to a wild goose chase," I say, with a smile.

"Yeah, okay, but this was different. I remember when Charlene went missing. I wasn't the journo to cover it at our end, but I remembered thinking the key to this case was here, not in Texas. No one actually saw her or spoke to her when she was supposedly in Austin. I tried to get my boss to listen, get me to ask questions at this end, but he wasn't interested. He thought it was a waste of time. So when you called, yeah, I thought, I'll take that one. It'll be a nice change from reporting on gardening shows."

"Well, good for you." I even clink my glass with hers, until I remember she's done me more harm than good. But then again, there's a part of me, a very small part of me, that knows it's not completely her fault. Everything she wrote is true, to a point.

"Considering Mike called you and admitted to the truth, although why he did that is anyone's guess at the moment, you must be pleased with yourself for following that hunch. He did have an affair, and he did pay her money to have an abortion."

"Yeah, actually Tamra, there's a couple of kinks there, but first I need to get something else to drink. This is disgusting." With a quick check at her cell phone, she slides out of the booth and makes her way to the bar.

I wonder what kinks she's talking about. And even more confusingly, why did Mike own up? To the paper, no less? What's happened to make him think it was safe for him to do that?

Fiona returns with two glasses of wine. "What did you want to show me?" I ask.

"The theory around Charlene's murder always centered on the fact that she went home to Austin. The police are having difficulties pinpointing where and when she died. Her body has been in the ground for almost two years. That's a lot of decomposition. But they still believe she wasn't killed that night, the night you drove her to the abortion clinic. They still think she flew back to Austin, and that she came back here soon after."

She stops talking but I don't remember hearing a question. I tilt my head. "Are you waiting for me to say something?" I ask.

"Well, does it sound right to you? Their theory?"

I feel myself redden a little. "Why are you asking me?" Then I immediately regret the words, knowing how defensive they sounded. I shake my head. "I'm just worried you'll use whatever I say for your next exclusive." I make air quotes around the word exclusive.

"Okay, I can see why you'd think that. But I'm not. You're the one who said you saw her get into your husband's car. You also said he had killed her. I'm asking you again because it seems I can't get a straight answer out of you on this one. Do you know for a fact that he killed her? That same night? Because I can't tell the difference anymore, between you revenge-rambling and you telling me facts."

She cocks her head at me. I take a moment. "What did you want to show me?" I say at last.

She sighs, gives me a look. "I'm coming to that. The morning after you took her to the clinic, Charlene went back to the house she shared and picked up her stuff. A few days after that, she took the flight that she'd already booked weeks earlier, back to Austin."

I rub a finger against the side of my glass, where the condensation has pearled and small rivulets are forming. I knew Charlene had supposedly used her plane ticket of course, because I poured over the news for months, waiting to see if she'd be found. I remember well the sleepless nights, the dread that I felt all the time, knowing I'd made a terrible mistake. I was sure the police would be knocking on our door, because she'd just finished working for Mike when she disappeared. He was nervous, too, back then. He seemed distracted. No, more than that, anxious. Tense. Spooked even. He asked me once, about a week after that awful night, how Charlene had seemed that evening. I figured he was worried I might have seen him, but it was such a strange question. I scoffed, and I just said 'fine, why?', as if he'd somehow challenged me. He didn't answer. I made the decision the next day to tell him every-thing. That I knew, that I'd seen what he had done. I wanted to tell him what I did. That I'd meant to help him, to protect him, to protect us. We would work out what to do, what to say, together. But then I found the news item online. Her family said she had come home, and then disappeared a day or two later. I didn't understand why they believed that. I remember for a moment thinking maybe she wasn't dead. That maybe she'd gotten up from her shallow grave, brushed herself off and walked away. I didn't really think that, obviously. But I didn't talk to Mike about it in the end, because no one came knocking on our door, and one day, I realized I hadn't thought about her in a while. After that, Charlene simply receded further and further away from my mind.

Fiona has stopped talking, but something she said earlier made me pause. I close my eyes, trying to capture the memory that's on the tip of my brain. Ah yes. I open my eyes again. "You said she went back to her house to pack her stuff, how do you know that?"

"Her housemate came home. Charlene had moved out

and left a note. It was agreed that Charlene would move out around that time anyway, so that wasn't a red flag in itself. Charlene took most of her clothes and asked that the rest be sent to her mother in Austin. She left money, too. For bills. She also sent a text the next day, a thank-you message."

I rub a hand over my eyes. My head is pounding. I can't do it. I can't think. Nothing makes sense anymore.

"You're shaking, you okay?" she asks.

I ignore the question. "Who saw her in Austin?"

"There are records. She texted her mother from the airport, from her own phone. We have CCTV images of her."

"You do?"

She nods. "At the airport."

I lean forward. "Can you get that? The CCTV footage?"

"I already have. That's what I want to show you. Because I had another good look, and I don't think it's Charlene."

Chapter Thirty-Eight

Of course it's not Charlene. When I first read that her family believed she had disappeared in Austin, I thought maybe she'd given her ticket away before she died. Something like that. I didn't know then, there was actual CCTV footage of her.

"What do you know, Tamra?"

Fiona is frowning at me. Did I say something out loud?

"Show it to me," I blurt out.

"Talk to me, Tamra. Tell me what you know, then I'll show you."

I don't think I have a choice anymore. "I already told you I saw Charlene get into Mike's car." She nods, but doesn't say anything. I take a deep breath. "I followed them."

And so begins my tale. I tell her how I saw him hit her with his car, and that maybe it was an accident, I couldn't tell.

"Fuck, Tamra! Why didn't you tell me this before?"

"Because I was scared," I lie. "I was afraid he'd find out I was talking to you, because who else could possibly have seen him, and not reported it? I was afraid of what he would do to me." Which is kind of true, I guess. She nods, and for now, I think I'm off the hook.

"So what did you do?" she asks.

I tell her the light version. The version that skips over the part where I buried her.

"I didn't go back to Greensboro for hours. I drove away, and I stayed away most of the night. I sat near the river and tried to make sense of what I'd just witnessed and what I should do about it. In the end I decided to go home and confront him. When I got back, the sun was rising. Mike wasn't home, but I was shocked to find that his car was, and in a perfect state."

That last part is true. It was astonishingly clean and without a trace of the horrible events of the night before. When he called me the next day, he was gentle and kind. "How did it go?" he asked, and I lost my breath in a shocked gasp.

"You know exactly how it went," I whispered.

"I can't hear you, babe. Can you speak up?"

I told him it went fine, that we'd talk when he got back. He told me again how sorry he was to have put me into this situation. That he would never forget it as long as he lived. That he was lucky to have me as his wife.

Is that how we're going to play it? I wondered.

Fiona remains still and silent for the entirety of my story. She can't take her eyes off me. Her jaw hangs slack —it even makes me laugh out loud, which is amazing, considering.

"Can I see the CCTV images now?"

"Okay." She rummages through her oversized bag, pulls out a folder, and slides a printed image in a clear plastic sheet across the table.

"Have you seen this one before?"

"No." I wonder how I could have missed it.

"That's the image that was circulated in the news when Charlene first went missing two years ago. I mentioned she sent text messages to her mother when she got to Austin, right? One from the airport, then another one later that day, from downtown. She told her mother she was staying with a friend and would come home in a couple of days."

I feel lightheaded, confused. For a moment I think maybe I buried the wrong woman. Then I shake the thought away. I think I'm going crazy.

"Did she? Stay with her friend?" I ask.

"No. The friend was real, but she hadn't heard from Charlene in months."

I'm so relieved to hear that, I let out a long breath.

"What's up? You know who this is?"

Fiona thinks my reaction has to do with this picture. I bend down to take a closer look. It's a woman with shoulder-length blond hair wearing a long dark coat. The image is head on, but it's blurry, grainy. From the little that I can make out of her features, sure, it could be Charlene, but then again, it could be any female between the ages of seventeen and thirty-five with blond hair.

Heck, it could be me.

"So?" she asks.

"Give me a minute." I didn't spend much time with Charlene. I picked her up from her place that evening, and I drove her for thirty minutes to the clinic. I'd be lying if I said I didn't pay attention to what she looked like. She had seduced my husband, was I interested? Damn right, I was. But it was dark, and I was driving. The best view of her I had was when she got in and when she got out. She was pretty, sure, no doubt about that. Was she so *breath-taking* that men's legs buckled at the sight of her, leaving them drooling all over her manicured toes as she twirled passed? I wouldn't have thought so. Unless you're my husband, apparently.

Fiona snaps her fingers under my nose. "Earth to Tamra?"

I flinch. "Please don't do that. It's really annoying."

"Sorry."

I tap the photo with my nail. "That coat is unusual." It's a long, double-breasted coat with a shiny edging and a fur collar. "Do you know for a fact that it's hers?"

She nods. "Her housemate confirmed it. Apparently, it's a cheap Burberry knockoff. She used to wear it all the time."

She wasn't wearing it the night I saw her. It was too warm, and anyway, I would have remembered. If I ever meet the housemate, I'll have to ask her if she knows where she got it. That's how shallow I am.

I'm sorry for your loss. Any chance you could tell me where she scored that Burberry knockoff coat?

"Do you have any other photos? I can't really tell with this."

"That's the best one, and the only one I had blown up. Here, let me show you." She grabs her phone, flicks her fingers on the screen, and hands it to me. "It's the best part of the CCTV footage. It's only two minutes, but she's too distant after that. Or facing the wrong way."

"Where did you get that?" I ask.

She shoots me a look that says, *you know who you're talking to, right?*

I watch the full two minutes without speaking, then I tap replay and zoom.

"So?"

"I don't know, there's something but—"

"There is?"

I peer at the video, then I catch it. It's not her face that gives it away, it's something in her gait, her demeanor.

"Holy crap, my God." My hand flies to my mouth.

"What is it?"

I press pause and the screen freezes, but this time she's side-on. I squint my eyes and peer at her profile. I tap the spot with my finger. My nail makes a light clicking sound against the glass. My heart is beating so fast it's making me breathless.

"Do you recognize her? Is it Charlene?"

"No. It's not Charlene."

"Tell me! Who is it?"

"Oh, God. I can't, I'm sorry."

"What do you mean?"

I snatch the printout and my bag and slide out of the booth.

"Where are you going?" Fiona asks.

"I have to talk to someone."

"Who?"

"I'll call you!" I yell on the way out.

Chapter Thirty-Nine

I'm in shock. The cold calculation of this entire tragedy is making my skin crawl. I should never, ever have kept my mouth shut back then. I am a fool, and probably an accessory to murder. But now, I know, without a shadow of a doubt, that Mike planned everything to happen just the way it did.

When I get to my house, I run to the door and press my finger on the doorbell. I have a key, obviously, but want to be able to see the shock on his face when he opens the door and he sees me, and I tell him that I know everything, and he's going to jail. I press the doorbell again, and finally the door opens.

"Tamra! I didn't expect you."

"Oh my God! Lauren! You don't waste any time, do you?"

She actually stands in the doorway, in *my* doorway, barring my way.

"What are you doing here, Tamra?"

"Excuse me? I live here, what the fuck are you doing here, *Lauren?* No, don't bother answering that," I laugh.

Bitterly? Damn right. "You can have him, by the way. He's a creep and a criminal and he's all yours."

She flinches at that. "What's the matter with you? Is that what all this is about? You ransack my house looking for what, exactly?"

"Oh wow, you're good. You're also wasting your time so get the fuck out of my way."

She doesn't budge. "Mike's not here. He's out of town."

"Is he? I want to see Madison. Can you let me pass? You're in *my* house!"

She steps forward through the doorway. She's only opened it enough so that she can fit in, and as a result I can't see inside. In her softest, almost conspiratorial voice, she says, "Yeah, look, I think it's best if you don't come in. She's really upset." She comes out of the house and pulls the door behind her, not quite shut, but almost.

"What are you talking about? What's happened?" I move to go around her, to push the door into my house, but Lauren blocks my way.

"Really, she's not ready to see you."

"Why?"

"Oh, God, where do I begin? Your association with the young woman, Charlene? You drove her? In your car? You've lied to Maddie about having an MBA, about your past, and when Maddie finds out about all of that, instead of talking to her, you just up and leave."

"Oh Christ, Lauren, don't do this!"

"Why? Because it's all about you? You have to understand, she feels let down. It's really hard on her. She finds out she has no idea who you are, then you cut and run like that."

"Oh Lauren, you really are a bitch."

"Next time, maybe give her a call first, you know?

Rather than just showing up unannounced." She puts her hand on my arm, and I almost hit her as I snatch it back.

"Fuck off, Lauren!" I storm back to my car, but not before I catch the glint of triumph in her eyes. When I turn around, she's gone back inside. I look up, and see Madison looking down at me.

"Maddie? Come down!" I yell.

She stares at me blankly.

I smile, beckon her with my hand. *Come down*, I mouth, but she turns away. Seconds later, a hand draws the drapes.

It's the first time I've called her Maddie.

Madison doesn't need babysitting, so if Mike isn't home, then I figure that Lauren would leave eventually. I park the car just off Fisher Park Circle on Carolina Street in a spot that gives me a clear view but also provides some privacy. I don't care if I have to stay here all night.

As it turns out, it's not all night. Just thirty minutes later her cute little BMW slides past me.

This time I don't try to break the door down. Just a gentle squeeze of the doorbell, and a few minutes later, Madison opens the door, her eyes wide at the sight of me.

"Hey, sorry about that before, with Lauren," I tell her. "How are you doing?"

She doesn't stop me, but she doesn't greet me with open arms, either. At least she lets me inside my own house.

She twirls a lock of hair around a finger, one foot on top of the other. "What's going on?"

"Why don't we go inside, okay?"

I make us a cup of hot chocolate. I haven't had one of those in years, but it's comfort food, I'm told, and right now, I need all the comfort I can get. "Lauren told me you're upset that I left, is that true?"

She makes a sound, like a snort. "You must be joking."

Okay, so maybe this isn't quite the answer I was hoping for. "The last few days have been absolutely insane, with the cops, and that stupid article in the Tribune." I take my stool at the kitchen bar and put down two steaming mugs, pushing one across to her.

"It's low-fat milk," I point out. "Hardly any calories, I swear." I smile, to show it's a joke, but she doesn't even look up.

"Did you leave those pamphlets in my room?" she asks. "For the treatment center?"

"I did."

"And you called my mom?"

"Okay yeah, I did. I'm really worried about you, Maddie. I know what pressure you're under, I'm worried you're doing yourself some damage."

She scoffs again. It's the only means of communication she has with me. I speak, she scoffs. At least she's here, with me, at the kitchen counter. Unbelievably, that's progress.

"I don't think it's any of your business," she says now, "But if you must know, yeah, I'm stressed. I'm studying, for real." She looks at me with an expression that says, *unlike some people*, and then she adds, "I guess you wouldn't know what that's like."

She really doesn't let up, that girl. I take a deep breath. "Madison," then, to soften the blow, I add, "honey," then I put my hand on her arm and finish with, "I know you've dropped out of Columbia."

She says nothing, widens her eyes, and I watch the blood drain from her face. "Does my dad know?"

"No! I didn't tell him. I haven't told anyone. That's a conversation that you need to have with your dad."

She's silent but her eyes are pleading. She begins to shake.

"What wrong? What's going on?"

Suddenly, without warning, she begins to cry a torrent of tears. In between sobs she tells me how much she hates the course. She's can't *stand* Business Studies. She *sucks* at it. It's the most *boring* thing in the whole world and she should *never* have done it.

"So why did you?"

"Because I wanted to be like my dad. I thought it would be something we could share, you know?"

You thought he would love you more, I want to say. I should have been a psychologist.

"I was scared that he would throw me away, like he does with everyone else, eventually. I thought if I could be as much like him as possible, then, you know, he'd stick around."

"Maddie, your dad adores you. He thinks you walk on water. You could do a degree in, I don't know, toilet paper design and he'd be proud of you."

That makes her chuckle, I think. Maybe it's a sob. I can't tell exactly.

"But you're going to have to tell him, like, as soon as possible. You can't keep lying to him."

"I know."

I've never seen Maddie so vulnerable. It's a strange feeling, I don't know what to do. I want to take her in my arms, but I don't dare. She'll run off, I think, if I try to get too close.

"There's another thing, Maddie, actually, it's the main reason I'm here."

I pull the printout from my bag and lay it on the kitchen counter. "This is you."

She blanches, picks it up to take a closer look. There's a slight tremor in her hand.

"No, that's not me."

"I wasn't asking."

There's a flash of something in her eyes I can't quite read. "Maddie…" I lay a hand over her arm. She doesn't flick it away. "Do you know why I had to leave?"

"No."

"Because your dad did something very wrong two years ago, that has something to do with Charlene Donovan's disappearance. I stood by him back then, and now, at the first hint of trouble, he has thrown me under the bus."

"What did he do?"

I hesitate, for a moment. "You'll have to find out anyway, maybe it's better if you hear from me. Your dad, he… he ran over that girl, Charlene. I'm sorry, Maddie, but he killed her. I think it was an accident."

Her eyes open wide, almost in slow motion. Then her hand flies to her mouth and she closes her eyes. I think she's going to be sick.

"I'm really sorry, but it's the truth, I swear. And he won't take responsibility for what he's done. I'm really worried that he's going to do the same to you. Not because he doesn't love you, obviously, but because he's weak, and he's scared. I know he asked you to take this trip. This is you, at the Austin airport, wearing Charlene's clothes. This —" I tap gently on the photo, "—was taken before you had your mole removed."

She touches her cheek quickly, right to the spot where it used to be.

"You need to talk to me. And a lawyer, too, but start with me."

"How do you know all this?"

"About your dad? I saw him."

"How? Where?"

I give a short version of the events, but I don't think she believes me. She starts to cry again. "Maybe it's *you* who killed her! And you're trying to blame my dad!" she yells.

Suddenly she's hyperventilating. It's actually quite scary. "Okay, try to relax, Maddie," I tell her, while I rummage around for a paper bag. That's what you're supposed to do I think. I can hear her behind me, it's an awful sound, the sound of someone having a panic attack. I'm throwing open drawers and cabinets and rummaging under the sink, but there are no paper bags. Then, all of sudden, it's over. Like one of those flash storms. Slowly. I turn around, she's pale, she has a hand on her chest, she's catching her breath.

"You okay?" I ask, my heart beating probably as fast as hers.

"I think so," she says.

"You gave me a fright," I tell her. We're like a mirror image of each other, my hand on my own chest. I let out a laugh, like a cackle. She goes to the sink and gets herself a glass of water.

I sit back down. I'm still shaken up, but I decide to ignore her outburst. "How did you get there?" I ask, tapping the picture.

She makes a face, like she's in pain. "Dad asked me never to tell anyone. He made me promise."

"Yeah, well, forget about that. Unless you want to go to jail."

"No! But I—"

"You can't keep secrets just because your dad tells you to! You're not a child, Maddie! This girl is dead! You have to tell the truth, you don't have a choice anymore."

She's thinking about it. It doesn't escape me that I kept secrets for Mike too. I'm no better than Madison. Although, he's the master manipulator. He's pulling the strings and we don't even know it.

"Dad asked me to go to Austin and pick up a package for him. He didn't want to entrust it to a courier, because of its contents. That's what he told me. I don't even know what was in it."

"Nothing precious, I'm sure of it. It was just a ploy."

"He gave me that coat, the one in the picture. But I could see it had been used. I didn't want to wear it. He said it was so that no one would recognize me. It had to do with work he was doing for the government, he said."

I have to put my hand on my mouth to stop myself from snarling. Work for the *government*?

There's a sharp noise from somewhere inside the house, and we both jump. When I look at Madison, I see that she's as scared as I am. What the hell is going on?

"Where's your dad?"

"He had to go to New York, he said he'd be back tomorrow."

With *her*, I bet. I can hear the wind outside, the precursor to a storm. "It's okay. It's the blinds upstairs. The window must be open."

She blinks, then resumes. "He gave me a hat and a pair of sunglasses. Then he gave me a phone. I asked what I was supposed to do with it, he said not to worry about that. Just to make sure it was turned on when I landed."

"He used a scheduling app. Clever. That's how he got those texts sent to her mother."

"Who?"

"Charlene's mother received two texts from Charlene's phone. One at the airport after landing, and one thirty minutes later from downtown."

"I didn't know."

"This picture," I lift the printout, almost push it under her nose, "is the picture that was circulated when she went missing. Didn't you recognize yourself?"

"But I've never seen it!"

"Don't you watch the news?"

"No? Do you?"

I shrug. "No." Obviously I did keep a close eye on this story, but not close enough apparently.

"I guess she didn't rate enough to make it to my Twitter feed," she says, without a hint of irony. Then, in a trembling voice, she asks, "Are you going to tell the police?"

"No, Mike will have to do that. He'll come clean about what he's done, I give you my word. You don't need to worry about anything. Please don't mention our conversation to him, okay? I mean that. He won't face up to what he's done, yet, but he will. I just need to talk to him first."

"What will you do?"

"I'll make him understand."

"You won't... hurt him, will you?" She gnaws at the side of her thumb.

"Jesus, Maddie, of course not."

Later, when I get home, I'm so wired that I can't sleep.

Fortunately, Joan is still up and in the mood for a chat. She brings us a bottle of something cold and two glasses.

"You know, that was the closest I've been to my step daughter. Can you believe that?" I tell her over a glass of sparkling wine.

"What brought that on? What did you chat about?"

"Maybe one day I will tell you, but not now."

"Oh dear! Of course, don't tell me the details. Some kind of crisis I assume. There's something about a crisis that brings people together, I find."

I nod. "I suppose you're right. You're on better terms with your husband now, aren't you?"

"Oh, yes, we're very good friends. We always were, until that—hiccup of ours. But with our children, too, somehow our family is stronger for it."

"That's a glass-half-full way of looking at it," I say. I don't know whether to admire her or pity her. But I know what she means. When Mike is convicted and goes to jail, as he will, surely, Madison's going to need all the support she can get. I'm already worried that she'll feel guilty about the part that she will have played.

Chapter Forty

I call Mike, and the sound of his voice when he picks up sends shards of sadness down my throat.

"Oh, Tamra, babe, where are you? I've been so worried! You okay?"

"We need to talk."

I hear the relief in his sigh, as if I were offering some kind of olive branch. "Anything you want, Tamra. Do you want to come here to the house?" So suave, so kind.

Such a bullshitter.

"No. I'm staying with a friend. I'd rather you came here."

"Who's your friend?" He blurts out. There's a note of surprise in his voice, but something else too. Disapproval. I'm trying to think of a response when he says, "What can I do, Tamra? To make things right?"

"Just come. Tonight."

"Anything you like," he says. I give him the address, then I hang up.

I sure hope I can pull this off. I place the small video camera Fiona lent me on the mantel. She said it was legal for me to record our conversation because I'm a party to it. Something like that. Joan is letting me use her living room so I spend the next thirty minutes testing the camera, positioning the armchair so that it is smack in the middle of the screen. That's where he's going to sit. I've got to get everything exactly right because I'm not going to let him go until he admits to everything he's done.

And then, I'll give it all to Fiona.

Mike is due in about two hours, and I pace the room and watch the clock. I try to read a magazine, but I can't take in a single word, and I keep starting the same article over and over. I force myself to sit still and breathe, to admire the pretty vase of snapdragons that Joan picked this morning from her garden. Then my phone chimes with a text. It's from Mike.

Hey baby, can I meet you at Lauren's house instead? She's gone to see Dwayne so we can have privacy and I need to stay close. Maddie's in bed with the flu. Same time, okay?

Well, at least he doesn't even pretend anymore. Come to Lauren's house! He must have told her that we're meeting up tonight, and they've arranged to meet their exes at the same time. Unbelievable.

I don't want to go over there, I can't believe that he would even suggest it. I'm about to reply, *No, fuck you, my terms or nothing*, but then I think of Maddie. She's old enough to look after herself, isn't she?

I give her a call.

"Hello?" she answers in a voice that sounds more like a whisper.

"Oh wow, you are really sick. How are you feeling?"

"Pretty shitty, actually. What's up?" She barely finishes the sentence before a cough interrupts her. It's muffled and far away, so I wait until it passes and she returns. "Sorry," she croaks.

"Do you have a fever?" I ask.

"A hundred and four."

"Oh Maddie, you poor thing. You're in bed?" This feels incredible. I'm having a normal, nice conversation with Madison, and she hasn't snorted once.

"Yeah, Dad's made me a hot lemon drink and I've got some vitamin C."

"Okay, you look after yourself. Stay warm, you hear?"

"Yeah," she croaks. "I'm not going anywhere."

"Good."

"Have you spoken to my dad yet?"

"Not yet, but soon."

"Okay." Then lower, she adds, "You haven't told the police about me, have you?"

"No, of course not. Don't worry, Maddie, everything is going to be fine. I promise."

She's silent for a few seconds, but I know she's still there from the labored breathing. "Thanks, Tamra," she says at last.

"You bet."

I swear it's the first time she's said my name.

I look at my phone screen.

Okay, same time.

And I hit send.

I still have a key to Lauren's house, and after I buzz the

doorbell, just to make sure, I use it. It's dark by now, and there's a chill in the air that makes the hair on my skin stand. Or that's what I tell myself.

I didn't expect the wave of nostalgia that assaults me when I walk in, and it's like a twist in my heart. Lauren wasn't just my friend, she was my *closest* friend, *and* my confident. I have spent many hours in this house, laughing and sharing and doing all the things good friends do, and I haven't grieved that loss yet.

But now is not the time, so I take a deep breath and get on with it. *Fuck off, Girlfriend. Not.*

I tell myself it'll be fine. I actually say it out loud as I flick the light switch and the overhead chandelier illuminates the room. Then I turn on all the lamps, one by one, so we have max lighting here. Finally I go and find the most expensive bottle of wine I possibly can, and pour myself a drink. I sure don't want to get drunk, but I need something to make me relax. I take my elegant wine glass back to the living room, sit in the armchair in the corner, and I wait.

This house doesn't have a porch. But if it did, I'd be sitting out there in a rocking chair with a Lever-Action Henry shotgun across my lap. It's that kind of feeling.

When I hear the front door open softly, my heart roars. I am so on edge that I almost drop my glass. I stand up quickly, expecting to see him.

But it's her.

Chapter Forty-One

"Maddie? You shouldn't be here! How did you get here? You'll make yourself really sick! Go home!"

She coughs, a sharp sound, but when I look at her face, I see it's not a cough. It's a laugh, like a bark.

"Oh, Maddie! You'll make yourself sick," she mimics. I recoil. There's something wrong with her, but it's not the flu. It's like she's all wired up, tense like a spring, her body vibrating at the slightest movement.

"What's going on?"

She walks farther into the room, and I see the gun in her hand. I feel like my insides turn to liquid. "What are you doing? Your dad is going to be here any minute, why are you here?" My lips are shaking, and the words come out thick, blurry.

"My dad is over at your friend's house right now."

"No, he's not, we changed the plans."

"No." She shakes her head really fast, looking down. "I'm the one who sent the text from his phone and then deleted it. And your reply, too. He's over there now, and he has no idea you're here."

My head is spinning. I have to grab the side of the armchair to steady myself.

"What's going on?" I stare at the gun in her hand. It's Mike's gun. But I hid it. I can see myself doing it. "Where did you get that?"

"I found it." She juts her chin forward. "So what? It's my house, I can look through your stuff whenever I feel like it." She looks back at me and strangely, she hands the gun over to me. Her hand is shaking so much, I'm afraid she's going to drop it. "I'm sorry, Tamra, but you're going to have to shoot yourself in the head."

I can't move. I can taste bile in my mouth. My head hurts. It's like a million electrical wires short-circuiting inside my brain. She hasn't moved, her arm still stretched forward with the gun in her hand.

I don't reach out for it. Not yet. "Why are you doing this?" I ask.

"Did you really think it was my dad who ran over that bitch, Charlene? This whole time, you thought he did that?" Her eyes are red, bloodshot. There are dark, purplish circles under them. She's so pale, she's almost translucent.

"I told you. I was there. I saw him."

"No, you didn't. You saw his car, it's not the same thing. Oh Tamra, man, when you told me, I swear I had to stop myself from laughing. You're really not very bright, you know that?"

"What are you saying?"

"It's all your fault!" she shrieks, tears running down her face. "It's you! Everything is your fault! I've never wanted you in our lives. You weren't supposed to be there! But you're... like a bad smell that's ingrained in the carpet. You just. Won't. Go. Away!"

My legs are wobbly under me. I lift a hand slowly, palm out, and I sit back down on the armchair. "What have you done?"

She bites at the skin around her nails and I see that she's drawing blood. "It wasn't meant to go the way it went, okay? Just so you know. And it was her idea, I swear."

"Whose idea?"

"Charlene!"

"You knew her?"

"Yeah I knew her. I met her online, through one of those beauty tips groups. And she was very pretty, don't you think?"

I just can't believe what I'm hearing. Is she asking me to answer that question? I just shake my head. "I don't understand."

"She was living in New York, so we started to hang out. I told her about you, about how you ruined everything. How you ruined my mother's life, and my life, and my dad just didn't care about us, not the way he used to. She and her boyfriend broke up and she had to move out. She was trying to get a job, make some money. She wanted to go to L.A.

"One day, she told me about this idea she'd had. This *brilliant* idea, she called it. She'd come here and work for my dad, as an intern since she couldn't do anything else, then she'd seduce him and pretend she'd gotten pregnant."

She watches me, to gauge my reaction I think. She gets her money's worth because I am beyond shocked.

"You can pick up those fake pregnancy tests on eBay for like, five bucks. We thought that a couple of months later they'd be married, lose the baby, then she could divorce him shortly after and walk out with some cash. All the while, obviously, you would have gone back to wherever crappy hole you came from."

If only. This whole plan is breathtaking in its naivety. I have to remind myself she was only eighteen or nineteen at that point, but still.

"She really went for it, let me tell you! Every trick in the book. The button that comes undone at just the right moment, the brushing a little too close, you know the drill. But he wouldn't bite. We'd almost given up when one night, they had to work late, and, well, one thing led to another and they had sex right there on top of his desk."

Her eyes are darting everywhere. Then she sits down on the arm of the sofa and lays the gun on her lap. I can't take my eyes off it.

"That was supposed to be the beginning of the end, but the next day, he took her aside and said it could never happen again. And he looked like shit. We knew it was over, so we faked the pregnancy, anyway, and asked for some money. I was going to make sure you found out, but I didn't need to, because he told her that you knew all about it. And even that you'd drive her to the clinic." She shakes at the memory.

I think back to my conversation with Patti. It dawns on me that she didn't know anything, not even about the one-night stand. But when she saw it in the paper, she couldn't bear the thought he had kept something like that from her. She wanted to pretend she knew all along.

"She wasn't pregnant?" I ask.

"No. The plan was that you'd drop her off and five minutes later, I'd pick her up."

"But... you weren't even here! You were back in New York!"

"I came back. I was here. I stayed at her place, the deal was done, I was going to help her move out and go back."

I'm stunned. It's hard to wrap my head around this information. "But I saw Mike driving! I saw——"

"I was driving. Dad was miles away."

I'm trying to think back—the car, the windows, they're partly tinted. "He had his cap on," I say, to myself almost.

"He'd left his Panthers cap in the car, I was wearing it," she says.

Oh God. I assumed everything. It was dark. I just saw a silhouette, my brain filled the rest.

"And that's where it was supposed to end. We'd split the money, and she'd go home. She had her ticket and everything. But then she started to rant and rave in the car that she found out that dad was going to run for governor, so she decided she'd sold out too cheaply. She wanted to double it. She said she'd go back to him the next day, tell him she didn't get the abortion, and she wanted another half a mil' to do it. I was supposed to drop her off at her place, but I didn't know what she was going to do, so I kept driving."

She stops speaking, lost in her own thoughts. She's a nervous wreck. I'm about to say something to calm her down, something soft and soothing, but she stands abruptly and I recoil farther back into the armchair. The gun is shaking in her hand, and it's terrifying. I should have grabbed it when I had the chance.

"We argued, like, out of control. I told her to forget about it, it was out of the question. She said she'd sell her story to the tabloids. They'd pay good money for that, she said. She was shouting, I was shouting, I just kept driving because I didn't know where to go. Then I remembered our old house was empty, and I could take her there, so we could talk, sort it out. But she ran out of the car and into the woods. I yelled at her to get back in, I couldn't even see where she went. I was so pissed. After everything I'd done for her! She was walking away with half a million dollars, and now she behaved like a diva? Screw her! She could find her own way back. I pressed my foot on the accelerator so hard it made the car skid, and I blasted out of there. Next thing I know, she's standing in the middle of the road." She presses the heel of her hand against her forehead, then she starts hitting herself. "I couldn't stop the car! There was nothing I could do!" She's sobbing, her breath ragged and sharp, like a child.

"Maddie…"

"I wasn't thinking! I was in shock. I never meant to kill her! I swear! But she was dead. I'd never seen a dead person before. I was so scared. I pulled her off the road and I hid her under some leaves and branches, then I drove away. I figured someone would find her, and they'd see it was an accident."

She gnaws at the side of her thumb. The gun is on her lap. Slowly, I stand and extend an arm toward her. "Maddie."

"Stop! Listen!" she yells.

"Okay, I'll sit down again, all right?"

She nods, the tears dripping from her chin.

"I was going to drop the car off back home, then wait the rest of the night in a diner and go back to New York the next day. But then I saw that I'd lost an earring, and I didn't know where. I was so frightened. What was going to happen to me? If someone found my earring? They'd know it was me, wouldn't they? So I went back, to look for it."

And then she looks at me, wild-eyed and crazed, and in a loud whisper she says, "But she wasn't there."

No. She wasn't. She tells me she spent hours looking for Charlene, but she couldn't find her. It was like a nightmare, something out of a horror movie. She left finally because what else could she do? God. We must have crossed each other, so close.

"I took Dad's car to a car wash and then back to the house. But I still had her bag. So I took my bike, the one you thought had been stolen, and I went to her place and took all her stuff, left a note and some cash. I stayed in a cheap motel on the edge of town and waited. Then I used her plane ticket and went to Austin. And now, almost two years later, she appears again! It's like I've gone crazy. She was gone, and now she's here!" She leans forwards and her whole faces distorts into a grimace. "I haven't slept for two years, Tamra. I can't eat. I can't think. I can't study. I look over my shoulder all the time. I see her on every street corner. I hear her voice in my head."

"Listen, it's okay, we're going to talk to the police, and—"

"No!" She jumps, comes at me so fast, I fear she's going to hit me. "You're the one who's going to get blamed for this Tamra. Everyone thinks you did it, anyway. You'll go to jail forever. I'll tell them that you killed her, that you told me everything." She hands me the gun, her arm shaking. Slowly, like she's a dangerous animal, I reach for it and gently take it from her. I let out the breath I've been holding.

"You have to kill yourself, Tamra. Otherwise you'll go to prison forever."

Except she's completely, certifiably crazy.

"Hurry up!" she yells.

"Mike—I mean, your dad and I, we're over, anyway. You got what you wanted, so you can let me go."

"No! I want you to kill yourself! And you're doing it here, in this house, because you're really upset! Because you think Lauren is having an affair with my dad!"

"How do you know that?"

She cocks her head at me. Like I should know the answer to that.

"Because I wanted you to leave us. I thought if you believed that they were having an affair behind your back, you'd go away."

"If I believed…"

"The blue panties, I took them. I put them in his pocket. And whenever she came by the house, I made sure to leave a note for you to find afterwards. Actually the first one, and this is funny okay? She'd left it on your windscreen. I just had to tear a bit off at the end, it said girlfriend I think, whatever. Anyway, it was perfect! After that I just imitated her handwriting!"

The first one. *Thinking of you. I've got your back. Love you*

The notepad. The pale yellow paper. I remember now, the bottom corner was torn off. *Love you girlfriend*. That's what it would have said.

"Every time Lauren came around, I'd make a big deal about how much I liked her," she says now. "I couldn't care less about Lauren, but it was worth it, just to see your face. Then I'd tell her that you were complaining about her. Saying mean things, like she thought she was better than you, because she had her own real estate business."

Oh God. I remember a conversation we had, when she offered to help me get my real estate license.

"Oh, and those flyers all over town? I made them! I didn't really put them up everywhere because if someone recognized me… that wouldn't work, would it. But I dropped bundles of them here and there. At Lauren's house, then I dumped some in the lobby where that journo bitch you seem to follow around all the time…"

She's crazy. She's off her fucking rocket. I've heard enough. "Listen to me! I—"

I didn't hear the door, but suddenly, Mike's here, like an apparition. He's standing in the doorway and his voice booms into the room when he shouts, "Tamra!"

Madison spins around. "Daddy?"

"Oh thank God, Mike—" I want to rush into his arms, but he's wrapped them around Madison who is sobbing on his shoulder.

"I was so scared, Daddy!"

"Give me the gun, Tamra." He's white as a sheet. His eyes wide and swimming in a mixture of fear and sadness. "She tried to kill me," Madison yells.

"No no no, Mike, listen to me. It's not like that!" I extend my arm towards him. He shoves Madison behind him. This is all wrong. I want to show him I mean well, I shove the gun in his direction. Small gestures, with my hand, but it looks all wrong. "Take it!" I want to wipe the fear that's like a cloud over his face. But then Madison darts towards me and suddenly she's got the gun.

"It's not what you think," I say again, but it's too late. The noise roars in the room. I bring my hands to my ears.

I'm on the floor. My head hurts. The rug is almost against my eyeballs. I have a surreal impression of falling into nothingness, and then Charlene Donovan appears, floating above me.

What have I done?

Chapter Forty-Two

I was told later that the cops arrived within five minutes. This is a nice neighborhood, so normally at this time of night, they don't have much to do. Thank God, I say, because that saved me.

When I woke up in the hospital two days later, they had a policeman outside my door. In case I ran away, apparently. That would be funny, if it hadn't been so tragic. I could totally see myself running down the road with bandages flying out of my head. It wasn't a serious wound, they said. I wanted to ask them, have you ever been shot in the head?

Mike hadn't been to see me, the doctor said, but who could blame him. He still believed me to be the villain at that point. I told the cop about the video camera behind the flower arrangement in the corner. I prayed to God that it had worked. And that it was still there. It was, and it had.

I've been told that Madison lost it when she found out she'd been recorded. But all I could think about was Mike. I was scared that he might hate me. That he might hold me responsible, somehow, because after all, I was, wasn't I? Madison did all that because she hated me. And then I covered it up, because I loved him.

It's all pretty fucked up.

Chapter Forty-Three

Madison only got eight months. It doesn't seem like much, but it was a first offense and technically, it wasn't murder. 'Hit and Run', they called it. Thanks to me, I might add. I'm the one who testified that it was an accident. I was there, after all.

I got two years. Hiding the body turned out to be way more serious than hitting it, go figure. But I'm not complaining. I could have gotten a lot more. The strange thing is, I didn't mind jail. I'd learned so much at the homeless women's center that I was able to help lots of women there. I studied, and I became a counselor. For real, this time.

Madison got out of prison and into treatment, thank God. She was diagnosed with various conditions, including bipolar, anorexia obviously, color me surprised, and I didn't remind Mike what I'd been saying for months, that something wasn't right. She wrote me a letter almost every day after she was released. She wanted me to forgive her, she said. All these letters contained a heart-felt variation of her regret and self-loathing for what she did, and what she tried to do to me. "I already know, Maddie, you've told me. I don't have room anymore for them." I'd very happily burn them in the trash in fact. Like I didn't make mistakes. "Just call me," I said to her once.

"But it's not the same. I want you to *know*. I want you to have it in your hand."

Lauren found it harder to forgive Maddie. She still doesn't trust her, and they're working on that. But she, too, has received a letter a day, telling of her sorrow for the pain she's caused.

I spent my seventh wedding anniversary in jail. When Mike came to visit me, he brought the present that was meant to be a surprise. It was our prenuptial agreement, amended to show that if we ever divorced, we would split everything down the middle. That's what he had been working on with John Moller. I am entitled to fifty percent of all the wealth he had accumulated over the years. He wanted to show me that he believed we would stay together forever.

It's taken a lot for us to begin to heal, both together and separately. I learned so much, about myself. That I couldn't believe, not truly, in my gut, that someone like Mike would love me for who I am. I saw an angle everywhere. If I'd talked to him about what I'd seen that night, heck, we'd be in a whole other story. But I chose to lie, and pretend, because otherwise, I'd lose him. What's funny is that he did the same. He never told me that he had waited for Charlene to claim her money, that half a million bucks we went through so much to get. That's when he became anxious. He thought she had changed her mind, maybe wanted to sell her story. He called the doctor at the clinic who told him Charlene was never there, but then again, that's what he'd paid him to say. Then he found out she went missing, and because that had happened far away from here, he figured it had nothing to do with him anymore. Maybe she'd pulled a scam in her home town and she'd been caught. I asked him why he never told me all that.

"Because I was afraid of losing you. I had made such a monumental fuck up. I'd slept with another woman, I'd dragged you into the whole mess after that. We needed to move on. Before I found out she'd disappeared, I really thought if she was going to pull some other trick on me. I thought it would be too much for you. I couldn't bear it if you left me."

Of course he never ran for governor in the end. He couldn't. Lauren told me he was almost catatonic for the first few months. Poor Lauren. There was no affair with Mike, obviously. Dwayne had left her for some woman he'd met at an insurance seminar. Apparently, *Crystal* was madly in love with him and thought he walked on water, and Dwayne liked that—what man doesn't—then regretted it five seconds later. By then it was too late. Crystal had moved with him to the Ballantyne, Lauren never wanted to see his face again, and everyone was completely miserable.

Anyway, they made it after all. They're back together after a whole lot of counseling. God knows we did the same.

I was let out after eighteen months. You can't imagine what that feels like if you haven't been through it. You want the light, you want your life back, sure, but you're also leaving behind people you've bonded with. People who have gone through the hardship of prison with you. That's harder than you realize.

Mike was waiting for me. I'll never forget it. He was leaning against his car, a bouquet of yellow flowers in his hand. He picked me up and he held me in his arms, and he said he would never let me out of his sight ever again. Not for a single minute. It's taken a while, but I'm learning that I am loved, just as I am. I don't need to lie, or to pretend, and I don't need to keep secrets.

Fiona Martin is on the payroll now, at the Tribune. She got a raise, a substantial one, so she can afford a baby sitter. She can pick and choose whatever story she likes. She's their star reporter.

Joan and I have started our own shelter for homeless women. It takes up pretty much all our time. Mike wanted to be the main financial backer, but I explained that there was no need. I've managed to convince Frank to part with half of his donations towards our program. He thinks I have something on him—I don't, but since it's for a good cause, who am I to disabuse him?

I wanted to call it the Charlene Donovan House, but her parents wouldn't allow me to. This is the hardest part for me, now that I have fully realized what I did. It was an accident, and I robbed a young woman of her dignity, and prevented her family from mourning properly, for years. I have to live with that. I'm hoping I'll get there, and I can still be a good person. So maybe this isn't a tale of revenge after all. Maybe it is a story of redemption.

Maddie's in medical school now, in Connecticut. She lives mostly with her mom, but she comes to us at least once a month. She's doing great. I'm so proud of her. We both are. She says she's going to be a pediatrician and work with children in third-world countries.

And next week, we're going on The Ellen DeGeneres Show together.

Acknowledgments

There are invariably many wonderful and generous people involved in producing a book, and this one is no exception. I feel very lucky, and I am deeply grateful to all of you.

Thank you to my fabulous editor Traci Finlay, for helping me bring out the best in *The Loyal Wife* and keeping me enthusiastic the whole way through!

Thank you also to Mark Freyberg for taking the time to answer my questions on the legal points in this story. Mark's generous advice has been invaluable, and needless to say any errors are mine.

Thank you to my family and my dear friends for their ongoing support and enthusiasm, and especially to my darling husband, just because :)

And finally, dear reader, thank you for choosing this book.